Alice Payne Rides

BOOKS BY KATE HEARTFIELD

Alice Payne Arrives
Armed in Her Fashion
The Course of True Love

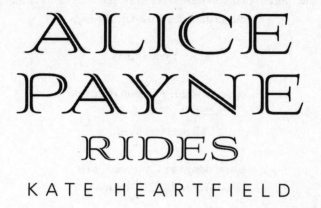

ALICE PAYNE RIDES

KATE HEARTFIELD

A TOM DOHERTY ASSOCIATES BOOK

NEW YORK

ALICE PAYNE RIDES

Copyright © 2019 by Kate Heartfield

Cover design by Christine Foltzer
Cover art by Cliff Nielsen

Edited by Lee Harris

A Tor.com Book
Published by Tom Doherty Associates
175 Fifth Avenue
New York, NY 10010

www.tor.com

Tor® is a registered trademark of

Macmillan Publishing Group, LLC.

ISBN 978-1-250-31376-8 (ebook)
ISBN 978-1-250-31375-1 (trade paperback)

First Edition: March 2019

For my parents, who taught me to work for a better timeline

CHAPTER ONE

By Which a Hostess's Intentions
Are Made Plain

1789

Alice Payne's dinner party fractures in the dessert course. She can almost see a fissure split the gleaming walnut of her new table, running between the plate of lemon cakes and the bowl of macaroons and veering catercorner to the custards. The footman (a glorious sensation, to have a footman at Fleance Hall!) pours for each guest, and Alice sees that they have chosen their factions.

Some drink port and talk politics: Alice herself, and Prudence Zuniga, the newest resident of Fleance Hall. Catherine Jenner, the youngest member of the party at twenty-eight years old, who has just come out of her first confinement. And at the far end of the table, next to Jane, Ambrose Duncan, the painter.

Some drink tea and talk science: her beloved Jane, of

course. Gertrude Lytton, seventy years old if she's a day, who has recently won a thirty-four-year inheritance lawsuit and can finally claim to own the house in which she lives with Agnes Bell. And Miss Bell, ostensibly Miss Lytton's companion, in much the same way that Jane is ostensibly Alice's companion. And the final tea-drinker is Edward Jenner, country doctor and polymath, married to Catherine.

"But how can we be *sure* that the king has recovered?" Catherine Jenner asks.

Mr. Duncan seems to assume that the question was directed at him, or at least that his opinion is the most germane.

"We never can be sure, but so long as His Majesty remains able to perform at least some of the functions of his office, all our Whig hopes for democratic reform must be tempered," Mr. Duncan says, and sighs, swirling the port in his glass.

"But what must that mean for the anti-slavery movement?" Mrs. Jenner continues, and all of the white-skinned people at the table very studiously do not look at Prudence Zuniga in that moment. It's a curious development; Alice, whose own mother was enslaved, is used to being the subject of averted gazes. But Prudence, being darker complected than Alice, being a stranger to Hampshire, has spun some invisible social orrery, changing all the angles of the glances.

"Nothing good, I'm afraid," says Prudence, with a little twitch at the corner of her mouth.

Alice's quizzical glance draws nothing more from Prudence, as usual. Prudence will seldom be drawn on the subject of the future. She protests that "the future" does not exist, that there are many possible futures, and that the future whence she came very likely no longer exists. Still, she sometimes gets a knowing look in her eyes that is irritating in the extreme, in combination with her reticence.

~

At the same moment as Catherine Jenner asks about the king, her husband Edward Jenner leans toward Jane, and asks, "But how can you be *sure* that the light itself was the cause of the needle's action?"

"The experiment must be repeated, of course," Jane says, with a slight flush to her cheek that Alice recognizes well. "But I have thought at great length about the affinity that underlies light, and magnetism, and electricity."

"You see some sort of occult connexion?" Miss Lytton asks, eagerly.

"Well, I wouldn't put it quite that way," says Jane. "But I do think—"

"My mentor always says a man of science should never *think*, but only *do*," says Dr. Jenner. "It is only through repeated examinations of the interior workings of the cuckoo, you see, that I was able to gain entrance to the Royal Society, and that only just this year. It takes many years of hard work to get anywhere in science, Miss Hodgson."

Jane sips her tea. "The Royal Society has made it quite clear that I shall not gain entry, Dr. Jenner, no matter how many birds I cut open."

"Of course," he says, slightly flustered. "Well, never mind about them, my dear. I only mean to say that reason must always be handmaiden to observation. I have learned a great deal by observing the simple country people, but if I am to convince the esteemed gentlemen in London of the truth of anything, I must gather evidence. They have yet to be convinced, for example, that a bout of cowpox in childhood can confer immunity to smallpox, but I have seen . . ."

"Captain Auden will be heartbroken to have missed this," Prudence whispers, leaning toward Alice so only she will hear, under the din of the two larger simultaneous conversations.

"Ha," Alice whispers back with a smile. "I think all his so-called investigating is a neat excuse. After all, we know he could be here at any time he likes. What is he off investigating today? The Princes in the Tower again?"

"Arthur of Brittany," Prudence says.

"Dr. Jenner, are you on about the cowpox again?" Mr. Duncan says, too loudly, and the table goes silent. Mr. Duncan is florid now, on his fourth glass.

"Forgive me," says Dr. Jenner, inclining his head. "My wife says that once I get in a rut, it would take a Clydesdale team to pull me out."

He says *my wife* in a way that makes it clear the phrase has all the luster of newness still to him, and he takes her hand.

"It occurs to me that I have not congratulated you on the birth of your son, Jenner," Mr. Duncan continues. "A new subject for your experiments."

"Not if I can help it," Catherine says, with a bright smile.

"A wife is a wonderful thing," Mr. Duncan goes on, as if no one had spoken. "A wonderful thing. The saviour of a man, I always say. Otherwise the passions of men miscarry in the most destructive ways."

"You make the passions of men sound rather horrible, Mr. Duncan," says Alice. She takes a few comfits, like tiny white pearls of rice, from her plate with a silver spoon. The sugared seeds brighten her tongue, benumb it just a little, as the earthy warmth of the caraway spreads through her mouth. She gently works the seeds between two molars, which helps her to say nothing more for the moment. She glances at the two old ladies, who seem likely to destroy Mr. Duncan simply by staring beatifically at him.

"Oh of course, I should not speak of such things to maiden ladies," the painter says, redder and louder now. "Women cannot understand it, of course."

"You think we are not capable of love, then, Mr. Duncan?" Miss Lytton asks, with a smile of glorious indifference.

"Oh, you mistake me. Why, Miss Lytton, you and Miss Bell are examples of the kind of love that comes naturally to women. A chaste love."

Alice and Jane catch each other keeping their mouths from twisting into giggles. But the two old ladies, who have shared the same household since George II was on the throne, simply stare at Mr. Duncan, their faces inscrutable.

"I have heard it said," Alice says, examining the port in her glass as if scrying, "that not all love between ladies is entirely chaste."

She doesn't need to look to the end of the table to know that Jane's fair face has gone pink. Alice delights in showing Jane how little she cares about the opinion of the world. And why should she care, now? Now that she has paid off Father's creditors, and Fleance Hall is a proper home, with a roof that does not leak, and a footman? Now that they can live as they like, and do as they like? For the most part.

Mr. Duncan makes a sound like a kettle about to boil. "I hope you pay little attention to the scurrilous libels in the London newspapers, Miss Payne. Certainly there are women who amuse themselves with Sapphic romances, but there is no true carnality in . . . playacting. It's a physiological impossibility, you see. Isn't it, Dr. Jenner?"

Dr. Jenner taps his teacup with his fingernail. "I am afraid most of my study of reproduction has to do with hedgehogs, sir."

"Ha," says Duncan. "Well, I'll leave it there. I see Mrs. Jenner is blushing. I forget I am not among my artistic friends."

Alice smiles at Catherine Jenner, who is in fact visibly amused, and opens her mouth to change the subject.

But Mr. Duncan has apparently not entirely tired of the sound of his own voice. He leans closer to Jane, so close that the razor-bumps on his chin very nearly brush her perfect cheek, and he whispers something that makes the muscles just under Jane's eyes contract. Jane stands, so abruptly that Duncan is thrown back, and Alice can tell from that exactly where his left hand was, the one that is not holding his glass.

Alice sits back, interlaces her fingers, save for the two

index fingers, which she holds to her lips. She gazes upon her beloved, thoughtfully, fiercely.

Jane raises her teacup, and says, "To the health of our hostess, Alice Payne."

Alice's lips smile, and her eyes send Jane an eternal message, a cipher for which Jane will always hold the key.

"Yes. To the mistress of Fleance Hall," says Miss Bell.

"My arse."

They turn, glasses foolishly in hand, to see Colonel John Payne standing in the doorway in his red silk banyan and brown cap. His eyes are red-rimmed but he is not drunk; his gaze is clearer than she's seen it in years. But he's shrunken from pain and illness, and the suspicion that was once a mere chancre on his character has now taken over his entire expression.

Alice walks to him, puts a tentative hand on his arm. "Father."

"You didn't want me at your party, Alice?"

"Your nurse said you were indisposed, sir."

"On the contrary. I feel very well indeed."

"That's the laudanum," she murmurs, but she turns to the company, puts her arm through her father's. He smells sour. "My father, Colonel Payne."

The company bids him good evening. "Will you take a brandy with us, sir?" Duncan calls out.

The Colonel steps eagerly, obstinately, out of Alice's

arm and toward the table, but his legs are unsteady. He turns back, looks at Alice's face. She does not try to forbid him or chide him. What difference would it make? There was a time when the Colonel was more cruel when in his cups, to please himself, but now he is cruel always, despite himself.

Still, he nods slightly, as though she's said something. He glances down.

"I am tired," he says.

"Let me take you to your rooms, Father," she says, softly, privately, but he shakes his head, and turns again and walks out of the dining room, back the way he came. Satterthwaite, his loyal manservant, appears in the door like a spectre.

The party breaks up quickly, after the old ladies take snuff and Dr. Jenner engages Jane in some headlong discourse about yolk sacs. As they watch Ambrose Duncan don his greatcoat and walk through the hall, Alice says to Prudence and particularly to Jane, "You see? I told you he was a pig. I had an intuition, but I didn't expect him to show it that way. Are you all right, Jane?"

"I'm fine."

"Teach him a lesson, Alice," Prudence says. "Auden has my shimmer belt, but you can use the time-wheel."

"Good," says Alice. "If only I had known, when I first became a knight of the road, that it was possible to be in two places at once." She checks the watch on the chain at her belt. "It's just a few minutes past nine o'clock now. I'll arrive at ten past on the hill. It'll be sure to catch him, and there would be no way I could have reached there first. I mean, in the absence of a time-wheel."

Jane nods. "As you like."

"You don't seem eager, beloved. And you had to sit next to the ass and his wandering hands all evening. I'm sorry about that, dear. If I'd known just how—"

"I only wonder what the point of it is. Yes, he'll have a fright, and lose some money. No one will know that we're the ones who did it, or why he deserved it."

"We'll know," Alice protests. She waves her hand at the far end of the hall, where the doors open from Fleance Hall out onto the world. "There is no justice out there. But here in this house"—she points her finger at the polished floor—"*in this house,* there will be justice."

Jane nods, but she says softly, "It seems a very small measure of justice, for such a large house."

CHAPTER TWO

One Woman Too Many

1789

Alice has so little faith in Ambrose Duncan's character that she is wearing her breeches under her petticoats. Once the gown comes off, the coat goes on, and the cocked hat and black mask. Around her mouth, her green kerchief, torn and speckled with the stains of her own blood. Her pistols at her waist, she goes out to saddle Havoc.

And with that, Alice Payne becomes the Holy Ghost, the most feared highwayman in Hampshire.

The first time Alice used Prudence's time-travel device out on the road, she considered going alone, without her horse. After all, she needed no conveyance to bring her from Fleance Hall to any part of the road—or the world—at any moment she wished. But Havoc is as much a part of her costume as the kerchief or the pistols.

She needs her gulls to *know* that she can chase them.

The trouble was that Havoc did not much like walking from one part of time and space to another, and would snort and quiver, and very nearly gave her away a few times. So Alice has had him go back and forth, through the shimmer, speaking softly to him and giving him plenty of breaks to canter on familiar ground.

Now, he faces the shimmer like a veteran, as Jane adjusts the time-wheel and a circle of strangeness appears at the stable door.

Alice never feels quite well herself when passing through a shimmer to another time and place—there's a moment of shock something like entering a cold stream, only without the cold or the wet—but she recovers, and Havoc stands brave and firm. They are on Gibbet Hill, overlooking Dray Road. *Her* road.

She can see, down below, the shapes of the old church, the dry-stone wall where Laverna, her automaton, once stood in wait. But Laverna has been dismantled now, her constituent parts added to the jumble in Jane's study.

She shivers in memory of the chill of that winter night, three months ago, when one of her gulls set a trap for her. Just as she was preparing to shout, "Stand and deliver," a man leaped from the old stone wall right onto Havoc's back. He had a knife, and he managed to cut her arm and slice the green handkerchief off her face before she knocked him to the ground and galloped away. He left her with the tiniest scar beside her ear—no one but Jane would notice it—but without her kerchief, and she was angry about that. How dare some nameless lout walk in the world with her kerchief?

Then she learned that the nameless lout had in fact turned it over to the parish constable, as evidence. And as the parish constable is her friend and neighbour Captain Wray Auden, Alice saw it again in his hands. He carried it on him, as a kind of token or reminder of the mystery he has yet to solve: the mystery of the Holy Ghost.

It rankled, that bit of stained green peeking out from Captain Auden's pocket as he bent over Alice's billiard table. It was hers, and she wanted it back. She used the time-wheel to enter his study while he was sleeping, plucked it from his desk, and now it is hers again. Torn and bloodied though it be, she refuses to wear any other, out on the road.

And Captain Auden's determination to lay his hands on the highwayman has only grown since said highway-man brazenly robbed his very home.

A small shape on the road from the direction of Fleance Hall; she puts a hand to Havoc's withers to calm him, though he shows no sign of moving or making a sound. But it is not her mark, not yet. It's Miss Lytton and Miss Bell in their phaeton. They pass her by, and she waits, unseen. The women left the party well before Mr. Duncan did, and though Mr. Duncan might go a little faster on horseback, he won't have overtaken them yet.

It's a fine night, crisp, but with very little moon. She hears Mr. Duncan before she sees him, riding his roan mare.

She smiles and presses one of the buttons on Jane's latest marvellous device.

As Duncan approaches a particular patch of the road, his horse rears. A plume of vapour rises from the ground, lit in such a fashion that it looks almost as though it has a shape, and that the shape might almost be human. Those two points of light, within, almost like eyes.

The second button, and a horrible wail sounds over the land. Just the wind in an open mouth of metal that rises from the earth a little way away, but the design makes it sound nearly human. Nearly.

"Christ!" Duncan screams. "What in God's name—"

The third button, and a circle of flames shoots up all around him. A dozen jets of fire, from hidden pipes in the earth. Jane nearly blew herself up in the making of this trap, but then she nearly blows herself up three times a week, and wears her scars with pride.

The mare screams.

Alice moves her leg against Havoc and they ride forward, into the light cast by the circle of flame. Another button, and all but two of the flames subside, so he can see her. *Let him get a good look,* she thinks, and is nearly tempted to pull down her kerchief. But she does not.

"Out of the road, rogue," says Duncan. "I won't be cowed by your sham."

"Sham?" she asks, her voice as low as she can make it. "The fire is real, sir. Ride through it if you like."

And she lets the flames rise again. His shoulder quivers, he turns in his seat as if seeking egress, but he makes no move.

She lets them die down again, and then he moves, kicking his horse, and she lets them rise up just as they're about to reach them. The mare rears and Duncan slips a little in the saddle.

Alice laughs loudly, but feels some sympathy for the horse, and vows to make sure she doesn't get singed.

"You shag-bag," she calls to Duncan, and lets the flames die down again, but only so they burn low, about to the horse's knees. "You rotten poltroon. Hand me your purse, and I'll be on my way, and you will have a story to bore women with at parties."

Duncan puts his hand to his belt then tosses something into the air. Although he's made no move and shown no weapon, she stays out of pistol range. She watches the bag fall onto the ground, and then she reduces the flames just low enough that he is able to induce his horse to step over them, and he rides away, coward that he is.

Alice depresses a final button and she's in darkness again, with no trace except the hoofmarks on the road and the clean, oily smells of Jane's fire-trap. It always reminds Alice of Jane's study, with its Argand lamps and strange spirits in bottles.

She rides closer, pulls out the telescoping handle of her riding crop (another of Jane's innovations), leans over and picks up Duncan's purse with it.

"Alice!"

She turns, hand at her waist, and sees Jane standing with a lantern, Prudence at her side, and behind them, a third person, entirely shadowed. In the darkness, she can't see a shimmer, but it must be there. All she can see in the lantern's golden light are the faces of her beloved and of Prudence, and those faces are grave.

"What is it? Is it Father?"

"It's motherfucking Wray Auden," says Prudence. "He wasn't just investigating. He was changing history. And all my safeguards failed, so we forgot."

"We . . . forgot?"

The third person steps forward, and Alice shifts so suddenly in the saddle that Havoc lifts his feet, uncertain.

The third person is also Prudence. A second Prudence. She is wearing a cloak; it's hard to say in the darkness, but it looks rust-coloured.

"We forgot," says that other Prudence. "When I checked my diary, and realized what happened, I shimmered back to the minute before he left in the first place. I prevented him from going. He . . . made other choices. Reasonable choices. Directed his energies elsewhere. It . . . I won't say too much, but it did not end well."

The cloaked Prudence looks up at Alice. She says nothing for a moment, but Alice remembers well enough what another version of Jane once told her, about what Wray Auden would do if he ever learned Alice's secret.

"Months later, we could see, in hindsight, where it all went wrong," the cloaked Prudence continues. "So we tried to rescue him from the moment he arrived in the thirteenth century. That didn't go well either. Not at all. We have been trying to save Wray Auden for a very long time now, and we know that there's only one moment when it's possible to save him, and everyone else."

"Everyone else?" Alice asks. The other Prudence—her Prudence—is scowling but silent. This is the sort of question she might ask; she already has, Alice realizes. Her Prudence has already been convinced by her double.

"We can't do it," Future Prudence says. "Not from our time."

"Why not?" Alice asks. "What's different, in your time?"

"Believe me, I wouldn't be here if it weren't our last resort," cloaked Prudence says, as if she believes that's an answer. "Bad things happen when you try to live your life over. Every teleosophy recruit learns that on day one. But it's the only solution I can see."

"We must go and save him, Alice," says Jane. "You will have to change your clothes."

CHAPTER THREE

One Woman Too Few

1203

There are few sounds in the dungeon. A faint trickle somewhere deep within or beyond the stone wall; the clinking of the chains whenever Wray shifts in a futile attempt to unknot his neck; the occasional moan from the dungeon's other occupant. Wray's mind forms words as bulwarks against the roar of silence, and the words are these: *What would Miss Payne do?*

He shakes the words away, with a rattle of chains. He ought to be able to find a solution within himself. He is Captain Wray Auden, parish constable and pensioned officer in His Majesty's service. He has been a prisoner before, and escaped before. That bitter march southeast from the battlefield at Saratoga. That long winter in the cold barracks. When the spring came, and the officers were paroled out to work in the fields with the old men and their wives and daughters, still he waited. When one of those wives offered to lie for him, that, at last, was his chance, and he took it, although it broke something in him to know he would never see her again.

Wray escaped, alone, and made his way to the nearest British camp, and to a promotion.

He must believe that if he waits, a chance will come, just as it did before. He has nothing but time, after all. There are five hundred and eighty-six years between this dungeon and the friends waiting for him in 1789.

By which time, he will be nothing but bones.

By God, Miss Payne *would* do something.

If he can just get one hand free, he can touch the shimmer belt that Miss Hodgson, in her practical way, adjusted to fit around his upper thigh, so thin that the guards did not find it when they patted him for knives.

One hand. That's all he needs.

He twists his head up, ignoring the complaints in his neck, and looks at the wall. There are two chains leading up from his wrists to the wall, each attached to a rusty iron bar. The mortar around the one on the right looks as crumbly as cheese. He strains against it, and thinks he feels it shift, give, just a little.

The truth is—and where can a man find truth if not in a dungeon—that Wray is no longer the man who waited all those years ago in that numbing barracks, and has no desire to be. He feels alive again, in a way he hasn't in a decade, and it's all due to the Misses Payne, Hodgson and Zuniga.

And if he doesn't get back to them soon, they might come looking. *That* is what Miss Payne would do. Put herself and her companions in danger, for him.

The fact that Miss Payne has not already appeared to extricate him is a puzzle.

The only explanation he can see is that he *does* arrive back where he is expected in 1789, the moment after he left. He must, therefore, succeed. He will succeed; he *has* succeeded, from a certain point of view. It's only a matter of doing it.

Wray strains harder, feeling the blood heat his face. The chain slackens as he rests. He pulls again, his wrists slick with sweat. This time, there is no doubting it. The bar is moving. He looks up, sees it wobbling.

What will happen if he steps through a shimmer into another place and time, with one hand still chained to the wall? He can't say, but he's soon to find out. From what Miss Zuniga has said, an object (or person) can exist between the two sides of the shimmer for only a few moments before being pulled to one side or the other. Perhaps the chain will snap in two, or be pulled clear of the wall and into 1789. That would be the best. If not, well. He'll step into Miss Hodgson's workroom in the eighteenth century, pick up a tool, alert his companions, and return to free his other hand and the youth.

He's known Alice Payne since he bought the house a mile distant from her father's, six years ago. He's always liked her company, and that of her pale, serious companion, Jane Hodgson. But it was not until after the arrival of Prudence Zuniga a year ago that he became, if he might be allowed the liberty, their friend.

Miss Zuniga caused a stir across the whole county when she came to live at Fleance Hall. The gossip was that she was Miss Payne's Jamaican mother, ignoring the fact that she is only eight years older than her putative daughter. Some simply assumed that she was another of Colonel Payne's unfortunate attachments.

Wray is no gossip, but it is his duty to know what goes on in the parish. That is how he learned that the women of Fleance Hall had a time-travel device. And that is why he finds himself in the year 1203, in Rouen Castle, next to Arthur of Brittany.

The youth moans. He's been insensible since yesterday. A fever of some kind? Some effect of the beating King John's men gave him? The boy won't survive another assault. Wray must get them both out of this dungeon.

He strains again, and three sounds break the dungeon silence:

First, an involuntary grunt from his own throat.

Second, a hideous clatter as the bar breaks free and hits the floor, the chain rattling with it, and the sinews burning in Wray's right arm.

Third, the patter of steps as the guards approach.

He gathers the chain in his hand and struggles to his feet. There's nothing for it: he can't risk opening the shimmer now, when the guards could follow him through, or pull him back by the chain. He'll have to get through this, and hope for mercy or luck.

The door opens.

Two of John's thugs; Wray doesn't know their names. That's good. They don't rank highly enough to kill prisoners without explicit instructions. Probably.

The one on Wray's right, nearest the broken chain, has a short ginger beard. The bigger one, on the left, is bald of chin and pate. They each draw short, one-handed swords.

He is in no position to engage them, no matter what weapons they carry. He'll have to take his punishment, wait for his moment, look for his chance.

The chance must come, he tells himself, or else Miss Payne would be here.

While the big bald one walks to Arthur and prods him with a booted toe, Ginger Beard approaches Wray.

"The dog's slipped his chain," Ginger Beard says with a cruel smile. "Not much good it will do you. The door's locked." He steps close to Wray, so close that Wray can smell the reek of his body. "Where do you think you're going to go?"

All those months Wray spent learning Norman French so he could bandy words with King John, and he ends up in close conversation with some thug whose name he'll never know. Of course, he did bandy a *few* words with King John. Enough to land him in here with Arthur.

As ever, Wray's grand sense of purpose has scuttled to a small and mean ending. Despair tugs down at the corner of his left eye like a tear, and up at the corner of his mouth like a tic. Like a smile.

Ginger Beard's eyes bulge and he raises his sword arm. As Wray's body reacts, ducking his head down into his chest, hunching his shoulders, some small analytical part of his brain manages to think, *So the pommel comes into use,* as the blow strikes the back of his skull.

All sound dissipates in the roar of blood and fear. He is not helpless.

Wray won't die here, by God.

He flings the chain out from his right hand, around Ginger Beard's body, and scrambles with his left hand against the small of the man's back. He can't reach the chain. He moves in closer. Ginger Beard's raised arm swings down, his forearm hard against Wray's Adam's apple. Wray's vision clouds. As he gurgles for air, the fingers of his left hand grasp the chain.

At last he has the man.

Wray cranks his head to the left, squeezes down out of the space between the man's arm and the wall. The stone wall scrapes his left ear bloody. He's squatting low, and pulls the chain tight around the man's knees. They buckle and Ginger Beard falls, messily, an elbow striking Wray's rib on the way.

Wray won't die here.

He twists the chain around the man's knees, hard, clambers on top of him, and slams the iron bar down on the guard's sword-arm. The man screams; Wray might have broken the arm. He puts all his weight down, to keep him immobile.

It's futile, he knows it's futile, but he can't stop. *Where do you think you're going to go?*

A flash in his peripheral vision and sharp pain in his wrist. The big bald guard has slashed Wray's arm with his sword and Wray automatically drops the chain, holding his wound, blood everywhere.

A crack of a whip and the sword clangs to the stone floor, and Bald cries out. Wray does not shift his weight on Ginger Beard's body but he looks up to see Bald holding his wrist.

And beyond, at last, Alice Payne.

Miss Payne stands in front of a shimmer in the air, a

mere trick of the light, one might think, if one did not know about time portals. She is not dressed for riding, but she holds a riding whip in her right hand. Her left hovers at her waist, where a leather belt holds a pistol at one hip and a mallet at the other. Somehow, this belt manages to look perfectly congruous against her pink-striped taffeta bodice.

Wray reaches for the sword that Bald dropped, shifting his weight as much as he dares on Ginger Beard's elbows and hips.

All three of the women have come through the shimmer from 1789. Miss Payne, still holding her whip. Beside her, Miss Hodgson, fiddling with a bit of paper in her hand.

Miss Zuniga, behind them, holds the time-wheel and surveys the dungeon with a soldier's eye. She crosses the floor toward Wray in a few brisk steps.

—and Wray is facedown on the floor, flipped over, his arm wrenched and screaming behind his back. Ginger Beard has him by the chain, and the worst of it is that Bald has picked up his sword and is lunging at Miss Payne, bent on revenge.

Miss Payne's whip cracks again, and curls around the sword as her lip curls in victory. But Bald has a better grip on his sword than she has on the whip, and when he pulls, it flies out of her hand.

Miss Hodgson, weaponless, steps between them.

At which point, Miss Payne draws the pistol on her belt.

"No!" shouts Miss Zuniga. "Alice, don't shoot!"

Miss Payne raises her hand and the butt of the pistol comes down on the guard's bald head and he stumbles past Miss Hodgson.

Miss Zuniga is at Wray's side now, and Ginger Beard's head is in the crook of her arm before he or Wray have any idea that is a thing that could ever happen. Miss Zuniga, who is half a foot taller and a good deal stronger than the guard, holds him as if he were a naughty child, and Ginger Beard drops Wray's chain to try to fend her off.

"Now would be a good time, Jane," Miss Zuniga mutters.

A good time for what?

"I can't—can't manage the—" Miss Hodgson fusses with the paper in her hand, and then her expression clears and she throws something into the middle of the room.

A crack of thunder and a flash of red light and the room fills with foul smoke. Wray is coughing, and next to him, Miss Zuniga releases the guard. He runs out of the dungeon with his companion.

Miss Payne kneels at Wray's side, with a green kerchief tied over her nose and mouth like a bandit. She sets her chisel against the link to the wall, and knocks it with the mallet.

"You must go," coughs Wray. "They'll be back in a moment."

"Hush," says Miss Zuniga, and she deftly ties a kerchief around his nose and mouth. It helps him breathe, a little, although it does nothing for the stinging in his eyes.

Miss Payne, on the other side of him, kneels and sets her chisel against the links near his shackle, the mallet in her other hand.

"You said," she says between her teeth and between chisel blows, "that as a royal prisoner, Arthur would be kept in comfort. You said he'd be riding horses. Eating almonds. On a curtained bed."

"So he was," Wray says, "until King John found out he was conspiring. He put him down here so his henchmen can mutilate him. We have time. You're nearly through already, Miss Payne."

"I've some practice with a chisel," she mutters, and then follows, quickly, "On occasion Jane needs someone to hold a tool." She glances up at Miss Hodgson and winks, and Miss Hodgson's eyes go wide.

Wray has known for some time that Miss Hodgson is more than "companion" to Miss Payne, but he has never quite thought of a way to signal his knowledge in a gallant way, so he pretends he doesn't know. Miss Payne, apparently believing he doesn't know, likes to tease Miss Hodgson by flirting in ways that he, Wray, might be expected to be too obtuse to notice.

"Quick, now," says Miss Zuniga. "Through the shimmer."

He shakes his head. "We can't leave the boy."

"Oh, for Christ's sake," Miss Zuniga says, throwing up her hands. The smoke has cleared a little, and no one is coughing now.

"Hardly a boy," Miss Payne says. "Sixteen, and he just led an army to besiege his grandmother."

The boy in question seems barely aware of his surroundings.

"Alice, they're going to gouge his eyes and—" He coughs, not entirely from the smoke, and now he knows he is going pink. "And they're going to wound him in other ways. So the barons won't want to make him king."

"And how did you end up down here with him?" Miss Zuniga demands.

"I, er, intervened."

"Of course you did." Miss Payne shakes her head, but she's smiling. "Jane, can you hold them off with another blast, do you think? If you hear them coming?"

Miss Hodgson nods, her mouth set thin, and pulls another wad of papers out of her pocket.

"We can't do this," says Miss Zuniga, with some futility, as Alice is already banging her chisel against Arthur's chains. "What's wrong with our little prince, anyway?"

"We planned to abduct him, you said," Miss Hodgson says. "And so we are. We were meant to follow Captain Auden, but we forgot, because he did something that changed history, and now—"

"But not like this," Miss Zuniga says, more angrily now. "We can't just go into the thirteenth goddamned century and start shooting people and disappearing—"

"I wasn't going to shoot him," Miss Payne says. "Just a warning shot."

"And leave a lump of eighteenth-century lead in the wall. We can't do this."

"We've done it," Miss Payne says, standing up and shaking the kinks out of her hands. "He's free. Should we leave him like this? Unchained, door open? So Arthur will escape, and he'll go off to become king, and it will be like we were never here."

Miss Payne, Miss Zuniga and Wray stand looking down at the boy, while Jane stands waiting in the doorway, listening for the guards.

Arthur of Brittany, but not King Arthur, not yet. By rights, he should have been king of England, as his dead father was next in line. But Arthur was a child, so the barons chose his uncle John instead. And when Arthur grew old enough to try to take some of his family lands by force, John captured him and his sister and shut them up here.

Then in the spring of 1203, Arthur escaped from the castle dungeon and made his way somehow to Paris. He bided his time. By 1215, the barons will turn on John and welcome Arthur as king. King Arthur. That's history. That's what happened.

And that's what Wray came here to change, to set in motion a plan to abduct the boy, drop him off in some time and place where he could do no harm, and change history so John will remain king.

Wray convinced them he was the best one for the indoor parts of the operation, being white (unlike Misses Zuniga and Payne), and experienced with fighting (unlike Miss Hodgson), and a man (unlike any of them).

But Wray fouled the whole thing up. Mentioned the escape plan to the boy within earshot of a hidden guard. Got himself into the dungeon with his would-be abductee.

The boy who would be king looks as though he's already had half the life knocked out of him. He hasn't even lifted his head. Sixteen years old, and about to lose his eyeballs, his testicles and probably his life's blood.

Damn it. Somehow, Wray doesn't think the boy will escape this time. History will change, but not as he intended.

Loud voices in Norman French, and the sound of dogs baying, the sound of people running.

"Now, Jane," says Miss Zuniga.

They all turn.

Miss Hodgson is not there.

The door is still ajar, and the guards are coming.

"Jane!" Miss Payne screams like a banshee, the mallet still in her hand. "Prudence, did she go through the door?"

"Go through the shimmer," Miss Zuniga says, stepping to the door and shutting it. "Now."

"I'm not leaving—" Miss Payne protests.

"She didn't go through the door," Miss Zuniga says. "So she's not here. Go on. We'll find her."

Miss Payne looks as if she could strangle her. "Surely—"

"Go!" Miss Zuniga shouts.

The guards are coming.

Wray grabs the boy Arthur by the wrist and pulls him to his feet. He puts the boy's arm around his shoulders and trudges over to the shimmer. The boy is walking, just barely, almost automatically.

Wray glances back at his companions, not asking permission. It is his fault that the boy is in the dungeon in the first place, and he'll be damned if he'll leave him there.

"Ah, fuck it," Prudence says, and pushes Alice through beside them.

CHAPTER FOUR

How She Met Herself

1789

Prudence follows the others through the shimmer, through the shock that sets her teeth on edge, still, after hundreds of times.

Back to Jane's study in 1789, to the creaking of wrought hulks and the dripping of cloudy stills.

Jane is there, her back to the others. She is staring at someone who is standing next to a shimmer, and the someone is the cloaked version of Prudence.

Prudence, from another time. Shit.

"You're still here," Prudence says.

Cloaked Prudence gives her a curt nod. "Not for long. Everything's good now, all right? Fixed. Don't go back and stop Wray from travelling. Don't do anything. Just . . . carry on." She waves her palms at them, as if she's doing a Jedi mind trick.

This isn't the first version of herself Prudence has met. She tries to avoid it. It's better, safer, to send someone else to deliver a warning, when a warning is unavoidable.

That is, after all, what brought Prudence here to 1789: Jane Hodgson travelled forward in time to warn Prudence not to try to destroy time travel for good. Sure, it had taken a while for Jane to convince Prudence that the outcome of that choice would be betrayal at the hands of her commanding officer and lifelong imprisonment, but eventually it had worked as intended.

Lecturers at the Academy relished the chance to tell the horror stories of their colleagues who had spent their entire lives reliving the same ten minutes, trying in vain to get it right. Both versions of Prudence knew well enough the stories of time travellers who wasted their whole lives trying to choose the time and manner of their deaths. Futures are so seductively infinite.

So Prudence had it drilled into her: redos are only for missions under orders, and for life-or-death.

And yet here she is, herself, staring back at her. A redo. So it's life or death, for someone.

"You yanked Jane through a shimmer," says Prudence. "Saved her life."

"My life!" Jane looks from one Prudence to the other.

Future Prudence nods, curtly. "It's done now. Don't go back."

"You knew this," Alice accuses Future Prudence, her hands two fists at her side. "You knew Jane was in danger if we went to the dungeon, and yet you told us to do it anyway."

"I told you it was the only way, and I wasn't lying," Future Prudence says, her voice strained, clipped. She turns to Present Prudence. "And I knew I could save her. And I did. This is the least shitty of all possible worlds, believe me."

"And what are we supposed to do with this asshole?" Prudence gestures at Arthur of Brittany, who is lolling against the feet of one of Jane's skeletons.

She does not like looking at her doppelganger, never has. It always makes her queasy, but it's worse this time. That Rossetti painting that hangs over General Almo's desk in the twenty-second century: *How They Met Themselves.* A man and a woman meet a man and a woman, identical except for the fact that one couple seems perfectly composed while their doubles are broken, distressed.

A painting that no one else in this room knows anything about, because it's 1789 here and now, and Dante Gabriel Rossetti has yet to swan out into the world. These people know nothing about the three-and-a-half centuries that yawn between them and Prudence's birth, and she's tried to keep it that way. Prudence has long

been a time traveller by profession; she is used to comb-
ing vocabulary and references out of her speech. But it's
exhausting. She sees her future self now in her mind's eye,
the way she will be if she spends the rest of her life living
among the people teleosophers call naïfs. Exhausted by
half a life spent not saying what she wants to say, because
her only friends wouldn't understand it.

Lonely.

Her actual future self shrugs. "You changed history.
He doesn't become king. That's all you should know right
now."

"I beg your pardon, er, Miss Zuniga," Auden interrupts, addressing the cloaked Prudence. He scratches his
temple to the accompaniment of a clatter from the chains
that still hang from his wrists. "I'm afraid I don't see how
history has changed. No one knows what happened to
Prince Arthur after the spring of 1203. That's the mystery
we were trying to solve. He disappeared. Everyone suspected John of killing him, but there was no evidence. As
far as history goes, Arthur has left the stage, just as he always did."

"That's how you remember it now, Wray," says Future
Prudence, her hands on her hips. "That's what you remember being taught."

She calls him *Wray*, not *Captain Auden*. What has
changed in this Prudence's life that allowed that to hap-

pen?

"Yes," Auden says, uncertainly.

Future Prudence smirks. Goddamn, she's insufferable. "You changed the past, which means you changed what's true. If you'd put in a note in your pocket about what you went in to do, when you came back out the note would say something different, in your own handwriting. Or it would be gone. Or it would be a lizard."

"What was our intention, then?" Alice asks. "Why did we go to 1203?"

Cloaked Prudence turns away, paces like a teacher. "We Farmers have always loved the Magna Carta. It's proof that progress can arise out of the competing demands of self-serving people. Small and slow. In the old timeline, though, it barely made a dent, at first. John had it annulled. The barons rode up against John and invited Arthur in. Arthur won. And King Arthur, who had much deeper and wider support than John had, had no need to make the barons happy. The Magna Carta was a mere blip, a first attempt."

"How extraordinary," says Auden. "I knew that changes in history could change our own recollections, but I would swear on my life I have always known that John remained king after the barons rose against him. He reissued the Magna Carta, and though he died not long after, his successors reconfirmed it."

"Thanks to you," says Future Prudence, pointing accusingly at Auden. "You got this boy out of the way. The effects downstream are pretty small, to be honest, but they're there. You changed the year of women's suffrage in three countries and several articles of the United States Constitution. But English history lost its real King Arthur."

"That's why Captain Auden went back," says Present Prudence. "We wanted to change history."

"I know you didn't remember that," says Future Prudence to the others. "Something happened—some change as soon as he arrived—that made us forget, made us believe that he only went to observe and investigate the way that Arthur escaped from the castle and rejoined his followers. But we wanted to get Arthur out of the way."

"It seems that is precisely what we've done," says Alice.

"No," says Present Prudence, rounding on her. She would like this accusatory edge to come out of her own voice but she can't help it. These people with their muskets and hair powder. They're completely unprepared for time travel. And whose fault is that? Prudence has failed again. She can see the accusation in her own eyes.

"Yes, Alice," says Future Prudence, her voice softer than the earlier version's. "You did it but you did it wrong. You meant to go back and abduct Arthur, take him out of

France and out of the picture, in a way that would look very much like an escape gone wrong. You were going to fake his death. Instead, you disappeared him. You created a historical mystery."

A historical mystery that will look like a flashing red light in space-time to a man in the future with a keen eye for meddling by time travellers. A mystery that could give General Almo a reason to come after Prudence.

And her future self told her to do it, said that the other ways were worse. *This is the least shitty of all possible worlds.*

She looks at her future self, opens her mouth to ask the questions she knows she'll regret asking.

"I'm going to go, before I fuck anything up," Future Prudence says. She steps through the shimmer and it dissipates, leaving no trace.

Prudence shakes her head, clearing the fears away. It must be fine, or her future self would have warned her. Right? Prudence may be an asshole but she can count on at least being a self-serving asshole. Almo has no way to find her, no tracker. He might know what she's done, but there's not much he can do about it. She'll just have to be more careful.

"I feel I'm not quite clear on the rules of time travel, still," says Jane.

Prudence turns to her. "My mentor at the Academy

used to say that time travel is like life: there are no rules, only consequences. The only rule is to always ask yourself what could possibly go wrong, and assume that it will. As in life."

Jane opens her mouth to reply—to argue, presumably—but Auden interrupts them.

"He has a fever," Auden says, his hand on the teenager's forehead. "A high one. No wonder he's in such a state."

"Jesus Christ. Step away from him and go wash your hands, Captain. Please."

She squats in front of the teenager.

He speaks, and she's shocked enough that it takes her a moment to understand what he's said. She's no expert in the pronunciation of the *langues d'oïl,* but it sounds sufficiently like "*où est ma sœur*" that she understands.

She stands and walks to Auden, who is scrubbing at a basin with a bar of lye soap, the chains making a racket. She whispers, "His sister?"

"Eleanor," Auden says. "Also in John's custody. She remains a prisoner for the rest of her long life, albeit a well-treated one." His expression clouds. "Or so I remember."

The teenager from the thirteenth century lets out a terrible scream.

"Blast him, he'll wake Father and frighten the servants," says Alice.

But Prudence is staring at the teenager, whose eyes are bugging out of his spotty face, whose mouth is so wide in his terror and anger that she can see the red spots on his tongue.

Smallpox.

Fucking hell.

She's been vaccinated, like every child born after the terrorist attack of 2054, when an early time traveller unleashed the virus in Manhattan and wiped out 30 percent of humanity. Unfucking that, while planting information to ensure the unfucked timeline would still have enough knowledge of it to vaccinate their children, was the first major mission of Teleosophic Core Command.

"Have you all had smallpox?"

Alice nods. "I had it as a child."

Wray says, "I did not, but I was inoculated, in America, during the war."

Alice adds, "Do you mean—has the boy got—but the servants!"

"And not only the servants."

They all look at Jane.

"You haven't had it, Jane?" Prudence asks, sharply.

"But you've been inoculated," Alice says. "That should be protection enough."

Jane grimaces. "I—"

Alice runs to her and takes both her hands.

Vaccination. Another way Prudence has failed to protect her new crew of time travellers.

She's been thinking about them as naïfs, not as colleagues. As part of the scenery. Smallpox is a hazard of their own time, no less than any other period to which they might travel. Still, she should have realized that popping in and out of other places and other times would put them at greater risk.

"Get her out of here, Alice," Prudence says. "Wray, quarantine the boy here. No servants come in here anyway. I'll be back in a moment."

"Here?" Jane blinks. "Quarantine him here?"

"For now," Prudence says.

"You're leaving? Now?" Alice glares at Prudence.

"I'm going to get something that will save Jane's life, and when I say I'll be back in a moment, I mean it. Go on, get her away from this room."

Prudence opens a shimmer and steps into the outskirts of Toronto in 2070.

CHAPTER FIVE

Being a Short Chapter, with Kissing

1789

Alice takes Jane by the hand and leads her out of the round tower study where her beloved spends most of her time.

"Don't touch that alembic; it has a crack in it," Jane calls back to Captain Auden. "In fact, don't touch anything."

Alice pulls the door closed behind them. Jane's study is the top floor of a round tower at one corner of Fleance Hall. It adjoins Jane's bedroom, and Alice keeps pulling her through it, away from the infected boy, toward the two dressing rooms that form a putative barrier between Jane's bedroom and her own. She and Jane usually sleep in Alice's room at the far end of the wing, where the bed is a little bigger, and the mysterious fumes from Jane's experiments can't reach.

Damn Captain Auden! She should never have agreed when Prudence recruited him to help with the adventures Prudence calls, with some pomposity, "the missions." Yes, Captain Auden had discovered Jane and Alice coming through a shimmer, but that could have been remedied some other way.

Alice must admit that Captain Auden's dogged pursuit of any historical mystery has served them well, and has distracted him from seeking the Holy Ghost.

And damn it all, Alice *likes* Wray Auden. She likes playing billiards with him in the evenings, while Jane tinkers and Prudence combs the Colonel's library. Auden doesn't talk unnecessarily, and when he does talk, his words tease out meanings like a card through wool. She likes his company and the quickness of his mind.

Still, there's a constant edge on her affection for him, like a black border of grief for innocence lost. She knows that Wray Auden would, in one possible future, take her to the magistrate and see her hanged for her crimes. A future version of Jane told her this. And she remembers her bloody kerchief, how he carried it with him, how he frowned over the mystery he could not solve.

She can't tell him the truth about herself, not ever, and so she can't let herself believe he is a true friend. He's a constant risk to Alice's freedom, and to her life here with Jane.

And now he's brought smallpox into their house, because Auden and his overdeveloped sense of duty would not leave well enough alone.

"This is ridiculous," Jane protests, pulling Alice to a stop.

Alice grits her teeth but stops pulling Jane through the bedroom, drops her hand.

"What is ridiculous," Alice says, "is that you have cajoled every one of our friends into buying an inoculation ribbon. You have written letters to the editors of every reputable newspaper in England and half of the disreputable ones. You refused to speak to Mrs. Greene after she said that inoculation wasn't safe enough for her precious children. And you have not been inoculated yourself?"

"You would know if I had been inoculated, Alice. I'd have been ill. I'd have a scar."

"I thought—I don't know, I suppose I assumed you had been as a child, before you came here."

"No. I meant to, my love, I did, but it never seemed a convenient time to have a fever—"

Alice throws up her hands and turns away, bites her lip. Here in the heart of the house, a new threat to keep at bay. She paid the last of Father's debts last month, telling him the money came from a wise investment. (It was not a lie, by a precise definition; the investment was in a tontine early in the century, in which the final surviving shareholder was to inherit the whole, and Alice managed to be present at both the beginning and the end of the arrangement, and a blackguard went to his grave unsatisfied.) She has no pecuniary need to go out as a highwayman anymore, and only does it to satisfy her sense of justice against the rakes and villains of Hampshire.

As for Col. Payne himself, her father has settled into a fairly steady state of detached, bitter bemusement. His rages now are few. She can keep him from wandering, most of the time. And on the few occasions when he's got out, she's been able to use the shimmer to retrieve him before he reaches the cliff edge, or the midnight road, or whatever peril he seems determined to find.

She has worked so hard to make Fleance Hall their own, their fortress, and yet—

"Why are you angry with me?" Jane asks, her voice quiet.

Alice whirls back to look at her. "I'm not." She means it. She's afraid she won't ever have the future she wants: A future in which every evening is spent in Jane's company, listening to Jane ask short, nervous questions in her husky voice while Alice inspects her strange inventions and experiments. In which every night is spent kissing the hollow beneath Jane's jaw and curling her fingertips in the hollow of Jane's hip bones. In which every morning is spent walking side by side in easy silence on the muddy footpaths of Hampshire, until Alice has worked the restlessness out of her limbs and Jane breaks the quiet by taking Alice's arm and pointing out some mushroom or nest.

She steps in close, runs her left hand along the downy hair at Jane's temple, down to the bun at the nape. The brush of her fingers at the back of Jane's neck arcs Jane's body like a bow.

"I need my study," Jane says.

Alice doesn't answer but kisses her, holding her shoulders, their bodices pressed together, the soft flesh above nearly kissing too. She tastes Jane's mouth as if for the first time, then pulls her golden head to her shoulder, tight.

She won't let any harm come to Jane.

A knock on the door, light, officious. The servants know to knock on these doors, upstairs. It's difficult to say whether they're more afraid of Jane's machines or of confirming some unspoken suspicion about Jane's relationship to Alice.

Alice smiles, and steps away from her beloved, and opens the door.

Satterthwaite's face is grave.

"My father," Alice prompts him. "Missing?"

He shakes his head, very slightly. "Miss Payne, would you like to sit down?"

She forms a fist with one hand, her fingernails biting into her palm. She can read the expression on Satterthwaite's face well enough. "Dead?"

"I regret—"

"Bring me to him."

CHAPTER SIX

In Which Prudence Talks to Her Sister;
or Not

2075

Prudence walks through Capsule, the tent city north of Toronto, keeping her eyes open. This is the most dangerous place in the universe, for her. So far, she hasn't seen any evidence that General Almo is looking for her, but if he ever decided to, this would be the place. It's the one place in all of history where Prudence can be guaranteed to show up: the place where her sister lives with her family.

Her brother-in-law Alexei is a nurse, when he isn't running contraband. He can get her the smallpox vaccine patches she needs, or tell her where to get them most easily. That's her excuse for choosing this particular piece of the future.

Prudence grew up in this place. It looked almost the

same in 2040 as it does today: the earth flat and brown, beaten by many footsteps, with little bits of wild chamomile or Queen Anne's lace in the small spaces between tents, at the edges of things. The tents themselves are the very worst shade of slug-beige, but every family has found some way to add colour. She passes one with what looks like a handmade clay gnome by the door, and another with rainbow prayer flags stretched across the entrance.

Even so, the overall effect is uniformity, stretching as far as she can see. There are letters and numbers painted on the tents, the only sure guide to a traveller looking for a particular family.

She's been trying to convince Grace to come back with her to 1789: the air is clean and the corsets are really not that bad. But Grace has refused. *You think I'm going to bring up little Nick in the age that produced Napoleon and Byron? I'm trying to raise a boy who's not an asshole, Prudence. Give him a fighting chance.*

So Prudence offered other times, other places. In theory, Grace and Alexei agree. 2070 is no place for a child, and they're ready to leave Capsule. But they've demurred when it comes to making a specific plan. They're not used to time travel, as Prudence is; the only time Grace has shimmered was in the mass migration of refugees that brought her and Prudence from 2140 to 2040 as children, and Alexei's never shimmered at all. They don't trust it, and they're angry at time travellers for screwing up the world.

There, at least, Prudence is forced to agree with them.

The tug-of-war between the Farmers and Misguideds over the course of history has become never-ending, each battle making the course of history worse. Prudence argued with her superior, General Almo. She pleaded with him to send her back earlier, to make deeper but more subtle changes. But he didn't care what she thought. Like everyone else, he was obsessed with the big moments, with changing the symptoms rather than the causes.

So in one timeline, she decided—would decide—to blow everything up. Maroon a generation's worth of Misguideds in the future, then disable time travel itself. And she very nearly succeeded, or so Jane said. Right up to the moment where Almo put her in prison.

Thanks to Jane, Prudence now has a chance to avoid that timeline. She got out. Deserted the army and went into hiding, to 1789. She may not have the resources that Teleosophic Core Command has, but she has two time-travel devices, years of training in propaganda and persuasion, and a group of willing noobs.

Sure, there was a moment when she was tempted to make sure that her enemies would never be born, but she's wary of messing with anything that could wink her own sister out of existence, since she knows from her diary that Grace doesn't exist in very many timelines. Prudence remembers every moment of their childhood together here in Capsule: how they played in the sandpit down near H753, how they made fans out of the propaganda pamphlets that the Misguided drones dropped overhead, to cool their sweaty bodies in the cinder-block classroom. She won't do anything that could let her sister vanish from history, from her own memory.

So she's gone rogue, but quietly. Gone back to first principles. Prudence is going to keep correcting history but she's going to do it carefully, do it better than the Farmers or the Misguideds and all their delusions of grandeur. Get the small things right, early.

The Magna Carta, for example.

She pauses, looks at a teenager leaning against a wall with nonchalance that seems a little too studied. Prudence has relied on time, not space, to evade anyone who might be looking for her here. She visits Capsule at nearly random points over a ten-year period, so that if Almo wanted to catch her, he'd have to post agents continuously for ten years, or get very lucky.

"Aunty Prudence!" A boy is running toward her, a four-year-old boy. She scoops her nephew into her arms.

"How are you, Nick?"

"I found a fossil. Just like you said. Do you want to see it?"

She nods, trying to keep her confusion out of her smile. He's referring to some conversation they'll have when he's younger. A conversation that is in the past for him, and the future for her. It's simultaneously disorienting and comforting: there's a possible timeline where she sees him again.

She glances back at the wall but the teenager's gone. It would probably please Almo to know that she's looking over her shoulder, wondering whether he's looking for her. And why should he bother? She's a deserter, yes, but wasting agents' time hunting her down would be throwing good manpower after bad.

She shakes her head, and takes the small, sweaty hand of a four-year-old boy who knows her better than she knows him. They walk toward a tent that looks like all the others, a core of sun-faded drab beneath a jumble of more colourful additions: a pink curtain drawn across the door, a rainbow whirligig stuck into the top of one pole. The address T30 in fading bruise-coloured paint on the fabric.

Grace comes to the door, squints against the sun, then puts her hands on her hips. "The prodigal returns. Come—"

~

—Prudence stands alone in the middle of Capsule and blinks for a moment, as if she's forgotten what she came for.

The vaccine, that was it. A camp for refugees from the future always has every major vaccine on hand, in case the horrors of the past resurface or are resurrected by imprudent time travelers. She needs to scope out the clinic, find out where exactly she should shimmer, and when. The clinic here at Capsule won't be well guarded. As good a place as any to get what she needs. Her childhood home, though there's no one here now she wants to see. Most of the friends she grew up with found their way either into crime or into the Academy, as she did.

The sun is hot and bright but she shivers all the same, and wipes sweat from her right palm.

Three steps in front of her, a brass plaque, stuck on top of a painted metal pole. An odd thing to find in a tent city. What could merit an official monument in a place built to relentlessly ephemerize the individual?

She steps forward, and sees an embedded black screen within a brass frame, and a single word engraved across the top: PRUDENCE.

Prudence freezes. Looks around, turning one slow, complete circle. A little girl with a rusty bicycle, and a skinny dog. She's alone, or close to it.

She examines the plaque more closely. On the right edge of the frame, a small oval depression. It looks like a fingerprint sensor. Did some future version of Prudence leave this here for herself? She has been known to leave herself notes, but a big metal pole with a screen on it doesn't seem like her style.

Fuck it.

She places the pad of her index finger on the sensor, then steps back as the screen illuminates.

General Almo's face fills the screen. She turns again, her hand at her hip, ready to shimmer out of here. She sees no one.

"Hi, Prudence. I hope you're doing well. We miss you."

He pauses, as if waiting for her to say something. Fat fucking chance. She looks around for cameras, but sees nothing likely.

"Of course," he continues, "we missed you as soon as you went away, but we understood. The pressure gets to everyone, and after so many failures in the Rudolf Project—what was it? Eighty? Ninety?"

"Seventy-one," she mutters.

"It's no wonder you wanted to give up. I thought that was all it was. But then, we noticed something mysterious in the historical record that hadn't been so mysterious before. A disappearance that we hadn't logged and investigated. Evidence of meddling. Evidence of you, Prudence."

He never used to call her Prudence. He called her Major Zuniga, but of course she isn't Major anything, now.

"It turns out you've been meddling with history," the man on the screen continues. "You ever read the Chesterton story 'The Hammer of God'?"

The pause Almo allows, when talking to a camera, is not much shorter than the pause he'd allow if Prudence were in the room, able to respond and be heard.

"It's about a man who spent too much time up in a belfry, and started to think of himself as being a kind of god, and the people below no better than ants. Time travel can be like that, I know. You see people's lives shifting, disappearing even, while you stay constant, or your brain tells you that you do. And you start to think they don't matter, not like you matter. And you find that you're lonely up in your belfry, and afraid. Afraid of what you might do."

No, she wants to say, and she even mouths it, silently. *No. That is how you feel, not how I feel. I'm afraid of screwing up but not out of contempt, never out of contempt. Don't assume your experience is universal. You always do that; it's your weakness as a general.*

"So you turn chickenshit," Almo is telling whatever camera recorded this message. "You're not the first, Prudence, believe me. You went AWOL. Big fucking deal, honestly. As long as you don't rub it in our faces, we're happy to let you be."

He rubs his forehead, as if genuinely concerned. "But we can't have you going rogue, Prudence. We've got enough on our hands with the motherfucking Misguideds. Come back now, and you won't be punished. I said we miss you, and I wasn't lying. You screwed up, sure. But you're a good agent. In fact, we miss you so much that we left you a little . . . sign. Something to show we care. If you check your diary, I think you'll find that you had a sister."

She pauses midscowl. A sister? She wants to ask him to repeat himself; she isn't sure she heard correctly.

"You won't remember her, I know. Take your time. Go read your diary—I bet you still have a diary somewhere in what we used to call prehistory. Her name was Grace, and she had a child. Your nephew. You loved her more than anyone. Now, you can ignore me if you want. Carry on. Live your life. After all, you won't remember her, so there's no real grief, right? Some people say they have sliptime dreams but I've always put that down to random neurons, myself. Still, maybe you'll dream of her. What do I know?"

He gives her his most kindly smile: 50 percent avuncular, 50 percent professorial, 100 percent asshole.

"If you do decide you'd like to have a family again, all you have to do is come home. Come to my office at noon GMT on November 30, 2145. One small change can bring your sister back, and you'll be welcome in the Farmers again. No court-martial and no questions asked. I'll wipe your record; I can do that, you know. If not, not. Suit yourself. You have stolen TCC property, and you've carried out illegal operations, and most of motherfucking *all*, you deserted us. This is your one chance—your one chance—to make all of that OK."

CHAPTER SEVEN

Concerning Colonel Payne

1789

Alice does not feel small in her father's library, despite her aunt's best efforts. When she was a child, and Col. Payne was seldom at home, she was forbidden from entering this room. Aunt Harriet, God rest her miserable soul, lost no opportunity to tell her so, with the tight set to her mouth that always accompanied any conversation with the illegitimate child Colonel Payne had brought home from Jamaica.

That child was meant to be a mere temporary inconvenience for Aunt Harriet. A few years of education in England, so that when Alice returned to Kingston, she'd be able to apply for "privileges," exemptions from the rules that prevented persons of colour from inheriting property or participating in the life of the nation.

But soon after Alice came to England, there was war in

Jamaica, as the enslaved tried to take back their freedom. Colonel Payne's estate there was burned to the ground.

One of her earliest distinct memories is of her father telling her that her mother was dead, and that they had nothing to return to, in Jamaica. It was a poor investment now, he said. A bad gamble.

He was going to buy a commission, he said. As a military man, he'd command respect, and there would be, as he put it somewhat darkly, opportunities.

So he went away again, and Alice would wait for his visits, for the presents he'd bring. In those years, before the war in America, he was kinder.

"Will your cousins try to take Fleance Hall?" Jane asks, interrupting Alice's thoughts.

"Hmm? Oh, probably. That's why I want to find the will, before we see the lawyer's version of it. I know he kept it in this desk somewhere. Have a rummage in that drawer, will you, dear?"

The library is round, in the tower that runs up one side of the house. Directly above it, on the top floor of the house where Alice and Jane spend most of their time, is Jane's study. She does not feel small in this room, not at all, though it is dim and dusty and smells faintly sour.

Alice cared for her father, not out of duty or even twisted gratitude for the man who brought her a doll every time he came home. She cared for him because he was old and sick and there was no one else to do it. And yes, now that he is dead, she wonders if she could have loved him better, in his final illness. It is a voice as brittle and obtuse as Aunt Harriet's, and Alice will put it away, just as she will take that dusty antelope head off the wall. She will keep the maps and the samovar. Order new fabric for the wing chair.

Jane is frozen, staring at a bit of paper in her hand.

"What is it?" Alice cranes her neck to see, but Jane turns it away from her view. "Oh, for heaven's sake." She snatches it out of Jane's hand.

She reads: *Know ye that I, John Payne of Kingston, Jamaica, do hereby manumit, set free and discharge from all further servitude the mulatto child Alice Payne, daughter of my Negro woman Mary . . .*

Alice hands the paper back to Jane with a tight smile. "I've seen it before. It's all right, Jane. Let's keep looking for the will."

Somehow it is always Alice who is reassuring white people that it is all right, when it is evidently the furthest thing from all right. Jane, at least, knows well enough to leave it there, and she keeps pulling things out of pigeonholes.

She won't find the manumission for Alice's mother, because it doesn't exist. If Jane finds any documents pertaining to the fifteen-year-old girl Colonel Payne enslaved and pretended was something like a wife to him,

Jane does not mention it. When Alice was a young woman, she used to tell herself that her mother did not die in Tacky's War but instead escaped and went to live with the Maroons, or took ship with Queen Cubah in Kingston and went to sea.

Alice at last puts her hand on it: a thick wad of paper, full of items crossed out and rewritten and crossed out again in her father's increasingly shaky hand. Lists of holdings in several countries, which may or may not now exist. She sighs. It will take a long time to sort through, and no doubt her cousins will contest it, saying that the Colonel was already of unsound mind when he wrote it. But at least the part about Fleance Hall is as clear as it could be: *To my daughter, Alice Payne, I leave Fleance Hall and all its attendant estate.*

Behind the wad of papers, there's a letter, small, folded, with a broken seal. Correspondence with a lawyer? She opens it, and reads:

To Colonel John Payne,

Sir, I write with sad Tidings of our mutual Friend, Captain Robert Greene. He died in his sleep, so says his good Wife, and did not suffer over much.

As for me, the Doctors say I have only a few months still upon this Earth, although I hope to prove them wrong at least until Christmas. I have been reading your last Letter over again and it strikes me that you have taken God's Judgment upon yourself for Actions in 1780, Actions whose full Import could not have been known at the time to any Mortal. It is Folly to imagine that your Orders on the evening of May 11 were the deciding Cause of the horrible Event four Days later and Hubris to sit in Judgment. There is only one Judge, and I go shortly to meet him.

In hopes of a reunion in that Glorious Land,
Your humble Servant,
Lt. Archibald Morse
"Or Glory"
Saint John, New Brunswick
Aug 22, 1785

Alice frowns, the paper creasing in her grip.

"What is it, darling?"

"My father had a letter. Four years ago. It makes reference to some horrible event on May 15, 1780. Do you remember what that might have been?"

Jane's brow furrows. "That was during the war. Horrible events were quite frequent, and of course we learned of them so long after they happened. If we saw some old newspapers—"

"My father kept a diary," says Alice, standing and rummaging in an open steamer trunk.

"Do you think he'd want us to read it?"

"I don't care one way or the other. I must live with his legacy now, the good and the bad, and if the old tosspot did something that could cause some lawsuit, I must know about it."

Alice finds the diary, its pale brown leather worn smooth, and flips through the pages. "Here we are. There's an entry for May 12, which reads only: 'Victory at Charleston.' The next entry is not until February of the following year."

She closes it.

"Sometimes I wonder whether I remember Father as being kinder and better before the war because he truly was, or because I was a child then, and unable to see just what a shite-hawk he was all his life."

Jane hesitates, then says, "My mother taught me never to speak ill of the dead. My mother is a superstitious woman, and wrong about many things."

Alice smiles despite everything, smiles at her Jane.

CHAPTER EIGHT

In Which Our Lovers Take
Each Other by the Hand

1789

Jane lets the warm weight of her hand be the conversation. When she first came to Fleance Hall to be Alice's companion, they sometimes walked hand in hand, or rested their heads on each other's laps as they read books and ate apples. In those moments, the world paled, and their pulses beat together.

It quickly became clear that Jane's *prospects* were not much better at Fleance Hall than they had been at home. Colonel Payne had hoodwinked Jane's mother into believing they would be. Jane cared little for *prospects,* anyway. She found an old telescope in the top room of the tower, and cleaned it and pointed it out the open window at the stars, and found it a very good prospect indeed. No one went into that room, except her, and Alice, when she was invited. Jane made it her own, adding whatever out-dated equipment she could purchase with her allowance.

When she was eighteen years old, Jane was courted. There was nothing wrong with William, which frustrated her to no end. He took her hand in his, and there was nothing natural or true in it. She refused him, and everyone said it was very sad. Baffling. A girl from a down-at-heel family, refusing a perfectly good proposal? A girl without *prospects.*

Then Colonel Payne went to war, and Alice and Jane settled happily into a quiet steadiness that survived his return. She can't say precisely when they slipped into the habit of resting their heads on each other's shoulders at every opportunity, or reaching out to stroke the other's arm out of affection, in the candlelit hours. How Jane interlaced her fingers in Alice's and leaned to kiss her cheek, as Alice sat on a sun-warmed stone bench watching Havoc graze. How they heard the Colonel coming up the stairs, raging at no one about nothing, and Alice put a finger to Jane's lips to say, *quiet,* and the finger remained, weighing Jane's lower lip, opening her mouth, moistening Alice's fingertip. Each of these caresses or grazes daring a little more, a little further, and yet still within the realm of *we are companions, we are friends, we are practically sisters.*

Why then? Why that summer week, two years past, after

so many years in the same house together? Once it began—whichever touch began it—the apotheosis seemed inevitable. The moment when Jane looked up from her microscope to see Alice bearing a cup of tea, and staring at her as if she were working out some remarkable puzzle. How Jane rose, and took the tea, and set it down, still face-to-face with Alice. How Alice took Jane's face in her two hands and kissed her. Only a brief buss on the lips, but a kiss that pushed the bounds of friendship to their breaking point, and then a gaze, a smile, and a second kiss, which Jane probably began although she doesn't quite remember. They broke three of her microscope slides that day.

How is it that Alice's hand on hers still holds all the mystery in the world, and all the certainty? It is a question she intends to keep asking, until all the bodies in the universe have cooled to a point of equilibrium and all motion ceases, that is, if Bailly's theories are correct.

The study door opens and Jane withdraws her hand from her beloved's. Prudence enters, with Captain Auden just behind. Prudence looks even more out of sorts than usual. She's carrying a bright orange box, molded or carved out of something not quite wood.

"Forgive us for intruding on your grief, Miss Payne," says Captain Auden. "Shall we return later?"

Alice bows her head. "Thank you, but this blow has been long in coming. I didn't know it would be a stroke that took him, of course, but I knew it would be something, before long. How is your Arthur now?"

"We've given the boy who would be king some antivirals, and I think he'll live," Prudence says. "He's sleeping comfortably on that little bed in Jane's study."

"Do you mean to say the future holds a cure for smallpox, as well as a preventative?" Jane asks, sitting straighter.

"Not a cure, but a treatment. They had some in the clinic where I swiped the vaccine, and I figured, in for a penny, in for a pound. Once he's cured, we can try to find a way to get him back to his own century in a way that won't set off all the alarm bells in history. Besides, I don't want to have to get rid of the kid's body. I hate digging holes."

Prudence seems as if she's talking half to herself, less careful than she usually is to be understood.

She opens the orange box and takes a small black spot out of it, holding it between thumb and forefinger. It's smaller and thinner than a penny. "I took a few dozen. Enough for any servants who might come here in the future, anyone else we might need to protect. Jane, could you remove your fichu and just pull down the shoulder of your dress? I think that's easiest. This can leave a small scar, I'm afraid."

Jane stands and complies, while Prudence touches the spot to her skin. It stings, and adheres.

"Is it osmosis?" Jane asks, peering at the site.

"Not quite. That little square contains more than a dozen tiny needles that scratch your skin and administer the virus. They activate with moisture," she adds, turning back to address Captain Auden, "so you have to be careful not to touch the needle surface. The darker side goes on your fingertip. Hold it to the skin for ten seconds. Once it adheres, the patient should leave it there for at least an hour. Longer is fine. All right? I'll linger close by in case you have any questions, but I think it's best if you do the servants. I doubt they'd be very happy having a black woman stick something on them."

Captain Auden shakes his head, but with astonishment, not refusal. "It's so . . . bloodless. Nothing like the inoculations I've seen. Will it work? And it won't make them ill?"

"Well, Jane, do tell me if you get a rash or a headache, but you should be fine. It's a much safer method than rubbing pus into wounds, let me tell you. It's not actually even smallpox virus, it's—" Prudence stops, glances at Jane's face. "It doesn't matter."

"It doesn't matter? You hold the ability to save a life on your fingertip." Jane stops to catch her breath, hardly realizing she's speaking aloud.

"When I was in America," Captain Auden says, and there's a slight hush, because he so seldom speaks of America, "I saw whole towns—whole peoples—sent to the grave. Children suffering."

"Surely we can . . ." Alice says, gesturing at the orange box.

"No," says Prudence, holding up a hand. "Stop and think. That smallpox that swept America during the war. If it hadn't, how would the course of that war have changed? You have no idea. *I* have no idea. You're talking about changing who lives and who dies, on a grand scale. Your own bloody English officers gave blankets infected with smallpox to Leni Lenape diplomats, for Christ's sake. So many ripple effects. You know what happens in the twentieth century? Humanity eradicates smallpox. Defeats it. What if that doesn't happen, because you all decide to change the course of history and give the vaccine to the governments of the eighteenth century? There's a brief window of public faith in international institutions in the twentieth century, and in that window, well, shit gets done. Would the Montreal Protocol go through? What would happen to the ozone layer? What about Bretton Woods, trade liberalization and the decline in poverty? You don't know. You don't even know what the ozone layer *is*. You're meddling in—you've already—" She stops.

Jane is used to being told she knows nothing of any importance. She is used to being just clever enough to be useful—to some great man of her acquaintance who needs a sympathetic ear or someone humble enough and clever enough to check his work—but not enough to be listened to.

"So Prudence Zuniga disposes," Jane says coldly. "And the rest of humanity lives, or dies, according to her decision."

Prudence shakes her head. "Every decision is life or death. Every goddamn decision. That boy in your lab lives; someone else loses a sister, or a brother, or a child. Listen. Trust me. In about forty years, a German scientist will figure out how to make a widespread, safe smallpox vaccine. Within your lifetimes, you'll see it. But you have to trust me. Small changes are life and death. Big changes are . . . misguided."

Jane opens her mouth to argue but Alice says, "The life-or-death decision at this moment concerns my servants. Captain Auden, do I understand that you're willing to administer the . . . What do you call it? Vaccine?"

He nods. "If Miss Zuniga will stand by in case I have need of her. There is a cook, a groom, a footman, your father's manservant, a housekeeper and a maid. Is that correct?"

"Yes. Six. They have all been told to ready themselves. If anyone objects, please send them to me. In the meantime, if you don't mind, I have many matters related to my father . . ."

"Of course," says Captain Auden, bowing his head.

They leave, Captain Auden holding the door for Prudence, who seems annoyed by it, but then she seems annoyed by everything and everyone today. No one forced her to come back with Jane-from-the-very-near-future to 1788, to make her home here at Fleance Hall. It was that *other* Jane's idea, and the Jane who was meeting Prudence for the first time could not very well object. She and Alice were both curious, in their own ways, both about the time-wheel and the woman from the twenty-second century.

Jane-of-the-future had left the time-wheel in their possession, saying as she stepped through the shimmer into her own world that if everything had changed as she thought it would, she would have a time-wheel of her own, in her own time. Jane spent an evening making notes and charts to try to make sense of it, to little avail. But now the occupants of Fleance Hall have two time-travel devices at their disposal: the belt that Prudence nearly always wears, and the time-wheel, a bit of brass a little like an astrolabe or a compass, with nine concentric wheels. It is remarkably easy to use.

And now it is in Alice's hand, and Alice is smiling at Jane.

"Where did that come from?" Jane asks.

"I took it from your study as we were leaving. I thought we might not want to return for it, while the boy is still ill. And now we have a reason to use it."

"You want to go to America. To 1780, to see your father."

Alice nods. "And look what else I have." She unfurls her left hand and shows three small black squares. "I took them while Prudence and Auden were intent on administering your vaccine."

"But what of Prudence's warnings? What of the consequences?"

"Everything has consequences. I don't think saving lives can ever be the wrong choice, and besides, I wanted to make you smile just as you are smiling now. You'll get a chance to look at these under your microscope soon enough, my love. In the meantime, will you come with me to America? I'll bring my pistols."

Alice's tone is as sprightly as it usually is when she proposes something rash, but it quivers strangely.

"What would Prudence say?" Jane asks.

"She would react as she does every time one of us has a thought of her own," Alice retorts. "Roll her eyes and bewail her fate. She's in a worse mood today than usual. I can't believe she'd approve, but I know she'd be wrong."

Jane takes the black patches and slips them into her own pocket so that she can take Alice's hand. "You know that I would go with you anywhere. To hell itself."

"Mmm, my love, that is no idle promise where I am concerned."

CHAPTER NINE

In Which Prudence Lies to the Servants

1789

Prudence slows her breathing as she descends the massive staircase, Auden following beside her. She feels beaten, and she does not respond well to feeling beaten. The first course of action after Almo's little gambit was plain and easy: get the smallpox vaccine back to her friends in 1789, and then decide what to do about her sister.

While Auden spoke with Arthur, she stepped into the little climate-controlled booth in the pre-Cambrian where she keeps her diary, and read about Grace. About all those lives in which Grace did not exist, and the ones where she did. How Prudence's own life was happier with a sister in it—how she chose to enroll in the Academy out of enthusiasm, not despair. The special school that Grace began for the children of Capsule. Alexei's face on the day Nick was born; the long hours that night when Prudence held the newborn Nick so Grace and Alexei could get a bit of sleep.

How *dare* Almo take all that away? How can he possibly believe there is any way in hell that Prudence would come back and work for a man who would do that to her?

No. Prudence is going to get her sister back, but she's not going to give Almo the slightest satisfaction. The problem is, though, how to do it, and then once she does, how to keep Almo off their backs.

They reach the door to the white parlour, and Auden, misreading her scowl, says, "I don't think they'll bite."

She gives him the least murderous expression she can muster, and they walk in.

The white parlour, on the ground floor, is not quite below-stairs but it is right beside the stairs that lead down to the servants' quarters, and the kitchen is just beyond it.

It's a very plain room, with old-fashioned plaster panelling, all vines and grapes. Alice told Prudence that it was her schoolroom, and Jane's, when they were still children. Now it's nearly empty save a long nearly white settee and an out-of-tune piano.

Half a dozen servants stand in a line, grim-faced.

Auden clears his throat. It's a delicate moment. Prudence will be damned before she pokes anyone with anything without their consent, but she can't have the servants spreading rumours of smallpox around the parish. On both those things, she and Auden have agreed.

"Thank you for coming. I want to be clear that this procedure is not mandatory. But for any of you who have not had smallpox, we want to offer this preventive measure. It is very safe. Much safer than inoculation. You almost certainly won't get sick from it at all. A small prick in the skin of the arm. And I must also tell you that we have reason to believe that people in Fleance Hall could be more susceptible to smallpox."

As they agreed, he leaves it there, letting them imagine what they will about Jane's experiments and the Colonel's travels.

"Does anyone have a question?" Auden asks.

Satterthwaite, the butler, coughs. "Begging your pardon, sir. Is this a device of Miss Hodgson's invention? I can't help but notice that Dr. Rhys is not performing the procedure."

Auden hesitates. He can't lie, bless him. He looks to Prudence, a liar of long practice, and she rescues him.

"What can you tell us about the medicine, Miss Zuniga?"

"These things must go through the proper channels, you know, and in London these days there are so many channels. Poor Dr. Rhys would be in quite a position if he were to administer any medicine without the Royal Society having a decade to debate it. In America, everyone has this done. I've had it done myself."

She smiles. It's almost entirely true. And she can see

their faces softening. She is still a propagandist. They trust her sincerity.

Prudence has always been particularly good at accents, although she doesn't have to work too hard in the eighteenth century. Outside of London, most English-speaking people on either side of the Atlantic still pronounce their Rs in 1789, and Prudence's native Canadian accent of the twenty-second century isn't too far off. She has to watch her internal Es and Is, and the cadences of her sentences, but she has a natural mockingbird tendency anyway.

And any differences, she puts down to the time she was said to have spent in America.

"Miss Hodgson made a wonderful false foot for my cousin after his accident," says the cook. "When Dr. Rhys said there was nothing to be done."

"Yes, she is a wonder, our Miss Hodgson," says Auden, smiling his gratitude at Prudence.

"Come to think of it," says Prudence, "I am due to have the procedure again, as the effects only last a few years. Captain Auden, would you be so kind?"

That *was* a lie. A spontaneous one.

"Of course," says Auden.

They didn't plan on this bit, but it works. The servants peer at them as Auden approaches, and Prudence pulls the shoulder of her robe à l'anglaise down, thanking the gods of fashion for the narrow shoulders of eighteenth-century dresses.

Still, she can feel herself blushing, for no reason at all, as Auden cups one hand around her shoulder and, too gently at first, daubs the patch on. She turns to inspect his work and sees his face closer up than she usually does. She barely notices that scar beside his nose, most of the time.

He's standing close, blocking the view with his body, and she wants to smack some sense into him. *Let them see! Be damned with propriety! They won't trust what they can't see.*

Then she realizes that he's spotted her tattoo, and that's what he's hiding from them. One more strangeness about Prudence Zuniga. Wise man. She'd nearly forgotten about the black seedling tattoo, its little roots spreading like veins. The sign of the Farmer. She went out for it with three other rookies, the night she got her acceptance message. She'd been prouder of this little bit of ink than of any grade she got at the Academy, and her grades were damn good.

A hot tear wells in one cheek, and she blinks angrily. Of all the moments. She's tired; her eyes are tired. And she can't wipe her eye now.

"There," Auden says, turning to the servants. "It's nothing at all. No blood."

In the end, the housekeeper, the maid and Satterthwaite agree to the procedure. The cook, the groom and the footman all claim to have had smallpox anyway as children, and perhaps they're telling the truth. She lets Auden be the one to administer the patches. Race theory is starting to appear in the late eighteenth century, and who knows what bile these people have been exposed to.

"At least we managed to do one thing without setting history on fire," Prudence says, as she and Auden are left alone in the quiet room. "Although, who can say? Perhaps we saved the life of someone who is bound to become the greatest monster in history."

"I would place my wager on the housemaid," says Auden darkly, and Prudence laughs.

She and Auden use the small serving staircase to return to the middle floor where the Colonel's study is.

"I beg your pardon," he says, touching her arm lightly on the staircase, "But you seem distraught, Miss Zuniga."

"Do I?" It comes out too brusque, but brusque is not so bad. "Well, we did kidnap an infectious king of England and lock him in a tower, so I have a lot on my mind, Captain."

"Of course. Would you permit me—"

"Yes?"

She stops walking, turns to look at him.

"The seedling, on your arm." He's a bit pink. "You may know that when I am not here, or about my business as constable, I keep a small farm at New House. I fancy myself a—well, I am no botanist, but I do make a study of plants, and I wondered what sort of plant it was. Perhaps something that grows in America? It was unfamiliar to me."

She grins, a real, spontaneous grin, despite everything. "You're wonderful, Captain Auden. I mean it. You make it hard to be a cynic. Hard, but not impossible."

His eyebrows bunch together. "You mock me, Miss Zuniga. Because I am a simple man and I like plants. All right, I admit it. I like plants."

"I like them too." She loses her smile; she can feel it vanishing, against her will. "But I can't keep them alive. I have no idea what kind of plant it is. Just something out of some tattoo artist's imagination, and then we all copied it. My fellow soldiers and I."

"I see. It's a bond not easily broken, I know. My regiment is called the Pattern, because it is known for being so well ordered, so disciplined. But you know what it used to make me think of? Knitting. A knitting pattern. And what happens when it unravels."

She nods, understanding what's underneath the words more than the words themselves. "Everything unravels. Time travel's hard that way. It messes with you, the inevitability of entropy. But you have to be able to see the beauty in the seedling. That's what the Farmers believe. Used to believe, anyway."

She looks, unseeing, at the bare walls of this staircase, walls that should be covered with paintings. Will be, once

Alice gets around to it. Things will change here. But she is here, now, on this step on this staircase. "I like plants too, Captain. I was reading my diary recently, and came across an entry about when I was a child. I had an herb garden in a pot, someone gave it to me for my birthday, a kit, you know. And the day after I planted the seeds, my sister found me digging them up, tears rolling down my cheeks. And my sister..." She pauses, swallows. "She asked me why I was digging up the seeds. I told her I was afraid that they wouldn't come up. I wanted to check on them, I guess. See? I told you. I like them, but I'm bad at them."

He nods, smiling kindly. "I didn't know you had a sister."

"I don't know whether I'll ever see her again."

"Ah. Well, the good thing about time travel is that everything's possible."

"Maybe."

He seems to understand that she doesn't want to talk about it anymore, and gestures with his arm for her to continue up the stairs, ahead of him.

They cross the gallery that stretches from one side of the house to the other, and she glances down through the arcade at the great hall, the heart of the house, where the Colonel's body lies.

They go through the old man's drawing room, and enter the study, and find it empty.

CHAPTER TEN

Where Alice Went Next

1789

Alice runs up to her rooms and brings down the breeches, shirt and boots she wears when she's a highwayman. She wriggles in, as Jane helps her out of her corset and skirts. Then she opens a cedar chest and pulls out her father's uniform jacket. The red wool and silver lacing have not dimmed, although the white of the facings has yellowed a bit. She throws it over her shoulders.

"Well?" she demands.

Jane cocks her head. "Aren't the breeches meant to be white? And I don't think those boots are right at all."

"But these fit me. I think anyone who gets close enough to wonder about my breeches and boots will have quite a few questions beyond that. I don't want to pass for a soldier, just not draw too much attention. Look, beloved, you haven't seen the best bit yet."

When Alice was a child, she thought the 17th Light Dragoons helmet was the most astonishing thing she had ever seen, and she has not changed her opinion since. It's a dome of black leather, upon which a brass crest rises like the prow of a ship, and out of the crest tumbles a plume of scarlet horsehair. Three inches of sheepskin line the bottom edge, and in front, a black metal triangular plate rising to a point in the middle, with a white skull-and-crossbones painted on it. It is as though the dragoons had been unable to decide whether to go to a masquerade as pirates or as centurions.

Alice ties her hair in a male style, with a black ribbon at the nape of her neck, and tries the helmet on. It is too big for her, so she takes her torn and stained green handkerchief and stuffs it into the helmet. It settles nicely, then, and she tucks stray tendrils into it. It's heavy, but not uncomfortable.

"There. Do I look fearsome?"

"I feel as if I'm about to be boarded," says Jane, putting her hand to her heart.

"Time for that later. Now, what about you? Shall we shimmer over to Auden's house and steal his old uniform?"

"I'll go as I am. Don't fuss, Alice. I've never heard of a war yet that didn't have women in it. I won't stand out."

Colonel John Payne loved nothing more than maps. On his rare visits home, when Alice was a child, he would show her maps of the world, the two round halves of the globe staring out at her like the gilded eyes of an owl, and the sturdy inhabitants of the Earth rising mostly nude from the bottom margin, or cherubs swooping entirely nude from the top. She would trace the trade winds with her chubby child's finger.

So Alice knows where to find the maps of America, the maps they need. They look at New York, and Boston, and Philadelphia, places that might as well be out of legend. Jane finds the latitude and longitude of Charleston, and Alice finds a smudged "Hart's Mill" on one of her father's hand-drawn maps in his diary, next to the crossed-swords symbol that designates a battlefield.

"The evening, the letter said," says Jane.

"The evening of May 11, 1780," Alice agrees.

Jane is not as practised as Prudence with shimmering, and the time wheel is much cruder than the belt Prudence wears, which has sensors that somehow read the intentions of the person pressing the button.

But Jane does her best to take them a bit wide of where she thinks the battlefield was likely to be, to reduce the chance that they'll be seen, walking out of thin air. To give them few moments of quiet to get their bearings.

Instead, they walk into the sound of gunfire.

CHAPTER ELEVEN

Where Prudence Went Next

1789

It takes Prudence and Auden the better part of an hour to search the house and grounds well enough to be sure that Alice and Jane are not there.

"But you do remember them," Prudence says, when they meet back in the hall, alone, their faces mirrors of each other's concern.

"Of course I remember them," says Auden, blanching, the freckles and scar standing out on his face. "Do you mean to say that you don't, Miss Zuniga?"

"No, I do," Prudence says, rubbing her hairline with the heel of her hand. "I do. Which means they're not erased from the timeline. But they're not here. And neither is the time-wheel."

"If they went to some other place and time—"

"They'd try to return back here the moment after

they left. Unless they weren't able to. Unless they're in trouble."

She's so angry she can barely think. How dare Alice go off half-cocked somewhere? And if Almo is somehow involved—

"Your diary, Miss Zuniga—"

"First place I checked. No clues there. We're not forgetting any plans. If they used the time-wheel, they did it without telling us."

Auden leans on a side table, taking some of the weight off his bad leg. "Why would they do something so foolhardy?"

"Ha, well, you know Alice," Prudence says, before remembering that Auden doesn't know many important things about Alice, including her double life as Hampshire's most notorious highwayman. She moves on hurriedly. "There's the question of where they went and why, and there's the question of why they haven't returned. And the second question, at least, I suspect I can find the answer to."

"That seems backward," Auden says with a frown.

"Welcome to time travel."

Almo wants to get her attention? Well, he's got it. She's sick of tiptoeing around him, anyway. Bastard. She'll find out exactly what he's done, and then she'll make him wish he never tried it.

She shifts her bodice up a bit so she can get at the shimmer belt. He steps toward her, but she holds out her other hand to stop him. "You stay here, Captain. I won't be a moment."

He shakes his head, but she's already opened the shimmer and steps through into 2145, where General Almo is waiting for her.

CHAPTER TWELVE

In Which Alice Is Foolhardy

1780

The moment they step through and Alice smells gunpowder she pulls Jane down into a crouch. They are behind a bit of old fence, and a foot away, a soldier lies, staring at the sky. The air is white with smoke or fog or both; she thinks she can smell the sea, under the electric stench of spent powder.

Alice can make out a dozen dark-coated shapes on the ground; the dead, or nearly dead. Shouting in the distance.

"No guns," Alice whispers. "I don't hear any guns. No drums. I think it's over, or nearly over."

"I can get us here earlier in the day. And farther away."

Alice leans forward as if sniffing the air. "It's May? You're sure it's May, in the evening? It's warm."

"It's South Carolina."

"Mmm. We're here now. Let's see what we see and then go back if we must. That shouting: that must be the victors, giving orders. I want to get a little closer."

"This may be the most foolhardy of the many foolhardy things you've done," Jane mutters, rising to her feet.

They stay low and within the trees that line the clearing. The ground slopes upward, and they can see a windmill breaking the mist on a low, bare hill, and the shapes of men and horses flitting around it. Three shots crack the air, and they freeze like rabbits; more shouting, but no more shots, and they move forward, toward the higher ground.

Ahead of them, on a ridge, a beaten dirt road winds to the mill. Men are running and walking along it. Most are in pale green coats but a few are in red-and-white uniforms like the one Alice is wearing, and they all seem to be comrades.

"Our side," Jane whispers, as they crouch behind a boulder. "We can't get any closer without being seen."

When Colonel Payne came home from the war, people spoke about the change in him, in tones of pity and dismay. It was not a change that anyone could have described, not at first. He had never been a steady man—not even a good man, truth be told—but now he was more bitter miasma than man at all. A cloud descended on Fleance Hall, and though it had no name, it was real and evident.

The effect of all of this on Alice was not in question. Of course the cloud was there, and of course Alice must live under it. *Poor girl.* Though she was twenty-seven years old when Father returned, and not a girl anymore at all. Men are storms whose effects women must not interrogate; the effects, like the men, must simply be borne.

But Alice will have no more clouds over Fleance Hall, not if she can help it. She will not have one of Father's secrets knocking on the door one day and hurting her, hurting Jane.

She turns to Jane and kisses her lightly, and smiles as the ridiculous helmet brushes against Jane's hair, pulling a golden strand onto the piratical plate. "You stay here. If I don't return by nightfall, shimmer home."

"No," Jane says, her expression grave and her hand on Alice's wrist. "You're not doing this."

"If I don't, I'll always wonder. You know I will, love. I'll try not to go out of sight."

Jane closes her eyes and lets all the breath leave her body before she nods slightly. Alice kisses her forehead, because that's the angle of kiss least likely to throw the horsehair plume in their faces or bruise Jane with the alarming brass prow of the helmet.

She straightens, slowly, and peers toward the road. Half a dozen soldiers in green coats and red ones, two carts, four horses. One man, on the road near the line where the woods end and the open land begins, has a musket drawn, looking out into the mist.

Alice strides forward with intention, hoping no one will notice the colour of her breeches. They are only one of several things wrong about her uniform, and then of course there is the matter of her sex. Still, if there is one thing she has learned on the road, it is that movement makes the man, or the woman. Every step is an offer, every stance a demand. From her calves to her shoulders to the tip of her father's ridiculous helmet, she wills herself to belong here.

And she thanks whatever gods control the weather in South Carolina for this fog.

The glances of the men on the road are casual, fleeting, as Alice passes them by, head just slightly low to convey the impression of some urgent errand and hide her face. But she looks at them quite carefully, if quickly. Scans their postures, their faces, their voices.

Out into the open land, where long skeins of electric-scented smoke have yet escaped the sun.

"Quickly now, quickly, lads. We may have won this skirmish, but there could be a hundred more across that creek. No time to lose."

She freezes. Her father's voice.

"They've as good as lost, sir," someone answers him.

"Charleston is burning, and by month's end, all the good Loyalists of South Carolina will be—"

"Look to your work, Corporal!"

Her father's voice, barking orders, does not yet have the querulous, desperate note she came to know in his final years. But it is his. She'd stake her life on it. He's turned slightly away from her, so she can walk behind him, hang back and listen without him seeing her. She maintains her occupied air as best she can.

Colonel Payne watches as three young men load muskets and rifles onto a low, one-horse cart.

"Some of these are loaded, sir," one protests.

"Then have a care."

"Yes, sir."

A man comes running past Jane, from within the woods, nearly bumping her shoulder. "Colonel Payne, sir."

They talk lowly for a moment, then her father lifts his head, lifts the selfsame helmet that Jane is wearing now. He looks past her, toward the tree line.

CHAPTER THIRTEEN

In Which Jane Is Foolhardy

1780

Alice has kept her word to stay in sight, but the mist out on the open ground transforms her into a dark shape. Jane risks standing a little higher to peer over the boulder.

Jane has never wanted to prevent Alice from going out on the road, or from writing essays or arguing with politicians or any of the other dangerous things she does. She would not be Alice Payne if she kept herself safe. But she wonders sometimes if Alice treats danger as its own reward, and if that might explain her faint, occasional reluctance to involve Jane too closely in her adventures. Alice would say, of course, that she is protecting Jane, but perhaps she's saving herself from examining her choices too closely, from the gaze of another.

Something moves at the end of her vision and Jane ducks lower. She peers toward the movement, not toward the hilltop with the living soldiers moving across it, but at the battlefield. In the mist, pale shapes move over the field but there are only a few and moving haphazardly. She puts her hand to her mouth to stop a gasp as she sees, so close that the mist does not obscure her, a woman. She is on her hands and knees, crawling, her gaze on the ground, her plain linen cap covering most of her hair.

The woman doesn't see Jane, doesn't seem to see anything but the soldier whose curly head she cradles.

And then, Jane takes a step back as she sees the soldier's arm flail, hears a long, loud groan.

The woman on the battlefield puts her finger to her lips, raises her face, looks around.

She's young—hardly a woman at all, Jane realizes, but just a girl. Her face is lined not with age but with anguish. The girl's eyes burn blue, the precise blue of Jane's late sister's eyes.

She doesn't see Jane. She's speaking to the soldier, whispering some long stream of words that seems more complex than mere platitudes to a dying stranger. And perhaps he's not dying. She's pulling long strips of linen out of her basket.

In the smoke beyond, Jane's eyes discern half a dozen figures moving. Standing, crouching, crawling, dragging.

A twig snaps. She crouches lower, turns. Two soldiers

in green coats are walking briskly toward her, their muskets at their sides. Do they see her? She makes herself as small as possible as the men pause just on the far side of the boulder.

"I don't know what you expect the colonel to do about it," says one of the men. "Charles King has already set sail for New York, and though he'll take a long route to dodge the French, he'll be walking into the Merchants in eight days' time, no matter what anyone here says or does about it."

"Walking into the Merchants and carrying smallpox with him," says a gruffer voice. "All those letters from the officers to their families, the bag that carries them. It was Albert Gray who collected them. And now Albert Gray is in quarantine for the bloody pox."

"I don't think they'd come through these woods anyway," says one, absently, as if hardly listening. "More likely on the far side of the field, over the creek."

"All the same, let's finish up here," says another, gruffer-voiced. "If another wave does come, and we fail to spot 'em, it'll be our hides. Hi—what's that?"

A rustle. Jane holds her breath.

"A redcoat. One of ours. Soldier! Lost your way?"

The familiar voice of the third man jolts Jane so that she nearly falls on her arse.

"I followed three of them into the creek," says Wray

Auden, sounding both more and less weary than the older Auden she knows. "They're dead. Made sure of it. They won't be fetching reinforcements."

"Reinforcements might come anyway," says the gruff-voiced man. "To you English lads it might look no different from any other place, but this is my own country. When the men die, they'll send the boys. They won't be cowed so easily."

"You sound almost proud, sir," says Captain Auden, his voice smooth as honey.

"I *am* proud. Proud when it's the king they're fighting for. When it's not, I know well enough to never let down my guard."

"*Whisht,*" hisses the other greencoat. "What's that?"

Silence for a few moments. "Something's moving out there. Look, another. And there."

"Women," says Captain Auden. "Women tending to the dead."

"Or readying their rifles," says gruff-voice. "Another thing you might want to remember about this war is that the rebels will take anyone. I've seen dozens of baggages and bitches toting guns or loading cannon in my time."

"I've been fighting this war from its beginning," Auden growls.

"Then you know," says the other.

"We have our orders," says the softer-voiced of the

greencoats. "Shoot anything that moves."

"I won't be party to—"

"You boys of the 33rd. The Pattern, that's what you call yourselves, eh? All book and no balls."

A metallic scrape—a ramrod in a bore.

Jane can't see Captain Auden's expression, but she can imagine it, as she hears the low chuckles of the other two men. She realizes first what has to be done, and second that she's the only one in any position to do it.

Captain Auden doesn't know her yet; he hasn't yet bought New House. He won't recognize her.

She backs away from her boulder as silently as she can manage, keeping low. Then she leaps to one side and runs toward the men at a fearful clip.

They have their backs turned to her. By the time they turn to her, guns drawn, it will look as though she's been running through the woods. She hopes. It occurs to her, just as the green-coated men turn their muskets on her, that moving toward a man who just loaded his musket while saying "Shoot anything that moves" is more foolhardy than anything Alice has ever done.

"God save the king!" Jane yells, raising her hands, and then, as a result, tripping on her skirt. She lands face-down in what is mostly moss, but scrapes her hands on a bit of old log and bangs her knee against something.

"Good God," says Captain Auden, rushing toward her

and helping her up. "Who are you? State your business!"

"I'm Mr. Lowell's daughter, sir," she says, adopting as innocent a tone as she can muster, and the careful, even syllables of an American. "He sent me to tell you that you're needed urgently. The rebels have attacked the camp at—" Blast. Damn! She tries to remember the names on the map, to think of a likely place where a camp ought to be, but she can't see anything in her mind's eye but musket smoke and the face of the blue-eyed woman. She lets her voice crack, and breaks into nearly real sobs.

"The camp at Sparling's Crossing?" says the soft-voiced greencoat, who turns out to be older than Jane expected, a jowly fellow with vague eyes. "Tell us, woman!"

She nods, grateful. "It's on fire," she says.

The gruff-voiced man, whose face is all cruel angles, looks out once more at the battlefield, then back to Jane. "If you're lying—"

"Come on, miss, you'd better tell this to the colonel," says Captain Auden. "First, please, have something to drink. That's a long run."

He offers her a wooden canteen. She is, in fact, thirsty, and tilts a few drops of the warm, tinny water into her mouth.

The men usher her forward, toward the road where their fellow soldiers are loading weapons onto carts. Toward Alice. Away from a decision that might have changed Captain Auden for good. Will they find a different Captain Auden in 1789 than the man they left behind? Or was the Captain Auden they know saved from this decision already in some way, or by some other version of Jane, for some other reason?

All in all, a worthwhile risk. She tells herself this, as she stumbles forward through the woods, ahead of these men and their loaded guns, toward their comrades.

Alice's father will recognize her, but perhaps she can convince him she only bears an uncanny resemblance to the girl he knows across the ocean. After all, there is no earthly explanation for why Jane would be here, and she is nine years older than she ought to be in 1780.

But the officer who comes striding toward them is not Colonel Payne, to her great relief, but a green-coated young man in a black-plumed helmet. He confers with Auden and the other men for a moment, then glances at Jane.

"Light companies ride to Sparling's Crossing," he says to the gruff-voiced man, who must be ten years his senior at least. "The infantry can finish loading the guns."

The green-coated men from the woods run off and give orders, and men on horseback circle and collect on the road, their horses whinnying.

The officer steps closer to Jane. "You'll have to come with us. Can you ride?"

"She can ride with me," says a red-coated soldier, trotting up on a piebald horse and stopping beside a rock, expectantly.

Jane studies the soldier's posture for a moment, then runs to the rock and swings up behind Alice.

"By all that's holy, are you a horse thief now?" she whispers, settling on the rolled blanket behind the saddle, wrapping her arms around Alice's waist. The coat still smells of cedar and dust.

"Who the hell . . . ?" the green-coated officer mutters, but Alice is already riding down the road, weaving in and out of the other horses as they ride to a camp that is almost certainly not on fire.

"I'm going to veer to the right on the count of ten," Alice whispers. "Are you ready?"

"But will the horse—"

"We'll find out."

Jane pulls the time-wheel from her pocket, sets it to the second set of calculations she'd made, back in the study.

"Ready."

"Nine. Ten!"

Their horse veers off the dirt road and into a beech copse and out of sight of the men on the road forever.

CHAPTER FOURTEEN

Of the Substance of the Horrible Event

1780

It's hotter, and not foggy at all, on the other side of the shimmer. The piebald mare rears and whinnies, and Alice pats its neck, calming it.

"Excellent," she says. "That was very well done. Very well done indeed. You are a mare of great courage."

"A mare some soldier will no doubt miss," Jane says.

"Hmm. Well, perhaps we can find a lovely situation for her. Where are we, Jane?"

They are in a narrow, cobbled alley between two burnt-out buildings. The smell of ash is strong, but there's no smoke, no fog, no gunfire.

"We're in Charleston," says Jane. "Around noon on May 15, if I got it right. Did you discover anything about your father?"

"Nothing. There wasn't time for much. We could go

back, earlier."

Jane takes a moment to answer, and when she does, her voice is unnaturally light. "Let's see what this day has in store for us. Perhaps if we know what the terrible event is, we will have more luck in finding its causes."

"Mmm," Alice says. It must have been difficult for Jane, alone in the trees like that. Truth be told, she doesn't have much stomach to witness the battle whose aftermath they saw. She lets the horse sniff the air, lets it test the cobbles beneath its feet. For the moment, she feels entirely herself and entirely comfortable, her legs comforting the horse, and Jane's legs comforting her. Jane's arms around her waist; Jane's left hand lowers a little as the right moves up, over the red coat that covers her breasts, and Jane's right hand grasps Alice's chin, tilts her head back. Jane's lips on her cheek, her ear.

"We don't have to stay here at all," Jane says.

A woman passes them on foot. She looks resentful, and with a small thrill Alice realizes it's not because she's recognized that both of the people embracing on the back of a horse are women. It's because of the red coat Alice is wearing, because of the fact that this city was under siege for weeks, and fell to the British only three days ago.

"Let's have a look around," she says.

They turn into a wider street. The place is noisy but not with the ordinary sounds of a town or city; there's shouting nearby, and someone is singing a song, not in joy but in mocking triumph.

Two gaunt children watch them from a doorway, one dark-skinned and one pale. If only she had something in her pockets—a few chestnuts, even. But she does not. Alice vows to return here and bring food—a bit of bread. Some apples, even some chocolate. She knows full well it's silly—there are uncounted numbers of hungry people in every time and place—but she's seen their faces, now, these two.

They pass a coffeehouse or tavern. It's deserted now, and clearly the conquering British had not yet got around to supplying it with food and coffee, as the only thing left on the trestle tables is a single hat. Over the door, a flag of dark blue, with a crescent in the corner bearing the word LIBERTY.

In a few years, Charleston will be part of an independent America. But today, these people know only that the British army has reasserted its might, its right.

A boom like thunder, and the horse screams, and bolts.

The houses shake and glass falls into the street.

Jane's arms tighten around Alice's waist as Alice pulls on the reins, brings the horse to a frantic stop, and stares at the great cloud of smoke rising from the centre of Charleston.

It's a pillar of fire, with dark objects flying out from it as if blown by a hurricane. Something whips past Alice and embeds in a window shutter; she turns to see it. It's a bayonet, stuck in the wood, shuddering.

"Good God," Jane says.

"All hands!" someone shouts.

"Fire!"

Alice slides down off the horse, her shin jolting from the quick landing, and helps Jane down after her. She pats the mare on the rump, to send it away, but the horse circles around her, nervous but not cowed.

The women run to a conduit nearby where a man is filling buckets. Alice takes one and Jane the other, and they run toward the fire, trying to go as quickly as possible without spilling the water.

"It's the weapons in the storehouse," yells a man running past, to no one in particular. "There's mountains of ordnance in there. Thousands of muskets. Ammunition. Powder. The magazine is on fire. Get out. We have to get out!"

Jane drops her bucket and takes Alice's hand, and they run with the crowd. As they pass a charred body, its limbs at unnatural angles, Alice puts her hand to Jane's head and pulls it toward her shoulder, guides her gaze away.

The piebald mare is still there, running but not in any clear direction. Alice runs to her and she slows.

"We take the horse with us," Alice says, and she leads the mare to a nearby stone and mounts, pulling Jane up behind her. She rides away from the explosion, back into the alley, away from the people. But no one is looking at them anyway. "Ready?"

Jane hesitates, again. She's fiddling with the time-wheel.

"Ready?" Alice prods.

"Ready."

CHAPTER FIFTEEN

On the Fragile History of Grace Zuniga

2145

Noon, November 30, 2145. But not precisely noon. Prudence deliberately arrives thirty seconds after the time Almo set, and manages to arrange her shimmer to appear behind the wood-and-paper screen that he keeps off to one side in his office. She has always suspected that he put the thing there to try to unfuck the godawful feng shui that comes with having an office with no door. There's only one way in or out of the place, and that's time travel.

This place has always made her nervous. But what choice does she have?

She sighs, and steps out from behind the screen, and takes some small consolation in his fleeting expression of surprise, the fact that he's halfway out from behind the desk, and not peering expectantly over it as he no doubt was half a minute ago.

"Ms. Zuniga," he says, with a hint of ironic familiarity, a hint of disdain, just enough emphasis on the *Ms.* to tell her that they've stripped her of her rank. Which she fully expected them to do, of course, but it stings nonetheless. "You decided to show up after all. I commend your good sense."

In the video, he'd called her Prudence. Was that him being good cop or bad cop? She leaves the shimmer open behind her. One step back and she can be out of here. Safe.

"Eighteenth century," Almo says, looking Prudence up and down. "The year is 1785, give or take. Am I right?"

She curtsies, holding her skirt between the thumb and forefinger of each hand, and raising her middle fingers. He responds with a joyless, brittle laugh.

"It wasn't enough for you to erase my sister," she says, the words *my sister* feeling foreign to her mouth, words she does not remember ever saying aloud before, "but now you've abducted my friends?"

"Abducted!" He scoffs. "I haven't abducted anyone. In point of fact, your *friends* were the ones who removed your sister from this timeline. Indirectly. Everything has consequences, Prudence. You knew that once."

So it's back to her first name after all.

"Tell me where they are."

He shakes his head, slowly, his gaze on her. "I believe if anyone here owes an explanation, it is you, Prudence. Tell me why you left. Why you *deserted*."

Over his desk, the painting of *How They Met Themselves*. Just as creepy as ever.

Prudence swallows. "I found out about a timeline where you screw me over. Sir."

He barks a laugh. "Good Christ. Was that it? You know as well as I do that we see the shadows of things that may be, not that will be. You threw everything away based on something I haven't even done? So petty."

He loves that Dickens quote. This is probably the tenth time she's heard it. She spreads her arms wide. "What can I say? I am a petty son of a bitch."

He concedes the point with a smile, a nod of his brown curls. He's thinner than last she saw him, or maybe she's just starting to forget.

"You always were good with details, that I'll grant. And it's true that the smallest change can shift the world. Take, for example, your own parents."

"What about them?"

"Ah, yes. That's why you're here, isn't it? In some time-lines, including this one, your mother once worked with a man named Marcus Larsen. Soon after she married your father. Never heard the name? No, she would not have mentioned it, would not have brought him home, not even as a colleague or a friend. And no, they never had an affair, in any timeline that we have seen. They were both far too honorable to act on their feelings, or even voice them to each other. But for six months, a year or two before you were born, your mother became, shall we say, withdrawn. She and your father—how shall I put this? They were not intimate very often, during those months. Your father never knew what cloud had come over their marriage. One day, it passed. Your mother chose to forget Marcus Larsen, chose to love the one she was with."

Prudence balls her fist. Her mother's private life, her emotions, are not General Warren Almo's sandbox. She's going to get this asshole.

Almo keeps talking, as usual. "Funny old world, isn't it? If Marcus Larsen exists, your mother falls in love. If Marcus Larsen exists, your sister doesn't. All your friends had to do, to erase your sister, was walk into one coffee-house and stop a murder. Not Marcus Larsen's, but his ancestor."

"You're telling me how I can get my sister back," Prudence says. *Where's the trap? There has to be one somewhere,* she thinks.

"No, I'm really not. I'm telling you why you're not going to. Not without my help. And for that"—he smiles, spreads his arms—"you need my forgiveness."

CHAPTER SIXTEEN

Which Shall Serve as an Introduction
to Charles King

1780

"The weapons," Alice gasps, as the mare snorts and stamps. "That's what my father regretted. Not taking more care with the weapons."

"But it might have been anyone, anytime," Jane says. "Thousands of muskets, they said."

Alice nods. "He thought it was him. Or he wondered—" She stops, looks around. They're not in Hampshire, or at least not any part of Hampshire she knows. They're in a town or city, on a beaten dirt street, with the screams of gulls in the air and the masts of ships bobbing in the spaces between buildings.

"Jane?"

"Yes, beloved?"

"Where are we?"

"New York City. May 19, 1780. We've gone ahead a few more days."

"New York City."

"When you left me behind that boulder—"

"I'm sorry, but—"

"I overheard some of the soldiers talking about a man named Charles King, who was carrying letters to New York. To the Merchants, they said. I remembered seeing the Merchants Coffeehouse on one of your father's maps. Wall Street, near the bottom tip of Manhattan, not far from the Battery. And look: there it is."

Jane's arm stretches out ahead of them, her finger pointing to a square building with a large sign over the door declaring it the MERCHANTS COFFEEHOUSE.

"And why do we care about this man and his letters? Is this to do with Father somehow?"

"I don't think so. But these men seemed to think the letters, perhaps the bag they're in, might be contaminated with smallpox. If we stop this man from going into the coffeehouse, and burn the letters, we might save some lives."

Alice breathes heavily, and the mare's ears flick back. Save which lives? Prudence would ask the question, and ask what the consequences would be. Will more people suffer, later, because of a life they save here today?

"I would like to do something good," Jane says, frustration in her voice. "I'd like to have some effect on something, even if it is only one life, or two, or three. I can't stand this constant . . . calculating, that comes with the time-wheel as Prudence would have us use it. We achieved nothing in Charleston, but we did learn one thing that might be of use to someone. I won't be a coward anymore."

Alice nods slowly. "All right, Angel of Mercy. Let us see what we can do here."

They tie the mare to a hitching stone, little more than a rough block with an iron ring set into one side. The horse seems almost calm, despite having gone through two shimmers in the last few minutes. A remarkable horse, mottled in black and white.

"I'll call her Magpie," Alice says. "My black-and-white horse who loves shimmers."

Jane makes a face. "You are taking her home, then?"

"I don't see why not. Havoc and Thunder could stand a little change, lest they become grumpy old men."

The blasted dragoon helmet is getting heavy, and Alice doubts it adds much to her disguise in any event. She takes it off. Across the inside of the dragoon helmet, a bit of leather stretches, a kind of handle. She runs the horse's rope through it.

Alice and Jane walk along Queen Street, toward the bobbing masts.

At first she feels self-conscious in her incomplete and imperfect soldier's uniform, but no one seems to bat an eye as she walks with Jane's arm in hers. In fact, she probably would have stood out more in the taffeta print she'd been wearing before they left, the bright peonies on yellow. Most of the women are wearing very plain cloth, solid whites and blues, plainer even than Jane's pink-and-white stripes. And of course, the women here are wearing the fashions of nine years ago, and an ocean away: long bodices or stomachers and short sleeves. Most of the skirts hang dismally beneath plain sashes or aprons, but an old lady of means sashays along in wide panniers.

They stand for a moment and look at the ships in the harbour. There are more than the three they saw from a distance, and all of them crawling with men loading, unloading, lounging, gossiping.

"Which one is his, I wonder?" Jane murmurs.

Alice shakes her head. "We could ask at each one, but we might easily miss him that way. We might have already missed him. What time is it?"

"Eight o'clock, if the time-wheel steered aright."

"Let's inquire at the Merchants. If he's already been and gone, we know we have to shimmer earlier. If he hasn't come yet, we know we'll meet him there. We'll stop him at the door and urge him to quarantine his ship."

"And if that doesn't work?"

Alice cocks her head. "As Prudence would say, then it's plan B. Whatever that may be."

Inside the ground floor of the Merchants Coffeehouse, their eyes adjust to the dim and din, to the smells of cooked meat and old coffee. There's a staircase at one corner, with men in very plain waistcoats and powdered hair hurrying up and down it, and lining each wall, booths made of dark, smooth wood, each one with a green curtain to close it off from the rest of the room.

At one end, a woman stands, quite evidently holding court by the way she stands and surveys. She sends a young man scurrying with a tray of steaming cups.

"We should pay for something, I suppose," Alice says, putting her hand into the pocket that isn't weighed down by the time-wheel. She pulls out two coins. "Just my damned luck. I've got a shilling and sixpence but they're both 1787. They'll think I'm a counterfeiter, and not a bright one. What have you got, Jane?"

"I've a '58 shilling. You're sure they'll take English money here?"

"Those are English uniforms, unless I've been much deceived," Alice says, glancing at a knot of red-coated soldiers lounging against one wall and drinking something more spirited than coffee. "And no one has run a bayonet through me and my red coat yet. Come to think of it, though, best if you do the talking. I'll hang back."

"Good afternoon, madam," says the woman as Jane approaches. "I don't believe we've met before."

"I'm Jane Hodgson," says Jane primly. It probably didn't occur to her to lie, or even to playact. If it had been up to Alice, they would have introduced themselves as . . . hmm, perhaps Cordelia Higgenbottom and Aloysia Spragg. Probably best it was up to Jane.

"If you've come from New Jersey," says the woman, stepping in closer, "you may be interested to know that the Chamber of Commerce is meeting upstairs as we speak."

Alice frowns. It's almost incomprehensible enough to be some sort of password, but she has the feeling it's meant in earnest.

"I can assure you I have not come from New Jersey," Jane says.

The woman makes a placating face and steps back again. "Fair enough."

"I have a meeting arranged with Charles King," Jane says. "Do you know if he's arrived yet in New York? I understood he would come straight here."

The landlady narrows her eyes. "Everyone of quality always does. Mr. King has not yet arrived, no, but I am expecting him today. The weather's been fair enough. You may wait for him here, if you like."

"That will serve very well," Jane says. "In the meantime, may we take one of those booths? And a plate of something?"

She gestures at Alice, who seems to be engaged in a game of scowls and appraising glances with another redcoat.

"It's sixpence each for a plate of cold tongue, cold ham, hot rolls and hot coffee," says the landlady. "You can take that booth nearest the door, and you'll be the first to see the man when he comes."

"Very kind of you," says Jane, paying her the shilling. "I have not met Mr. King in person before. I don't suppose you could tell me—"

The landlady holds her sides and chuckles. "I hardly know how to prepare you. He's... Well now. A bit of a macaroni, I suppose you'd say. Decked out in all the colours of the rainbow, likely. Quite the sight. I don't think you'll miss him."

"I'm in your debt, madam."

They sit on one side of the booth in the quietest part of the hall.

"What do you think counts as a macaroni, here?" Alice asks, looking around at the men in the room, who are either in well-worn uniforms or in dowdy browns.

"I suppose we'll find out," Jane says.

The tongue is boiled, served in cold pale slices with a

bit of pepper, and the rolls are fresh and hot. The coffee is bitter and muddy, but certainly stimulating. Alice and Jane are the only women other than the landlady.

"Did your father never speak of the explosion?"

Alice looks down at her plate. "He hardly spoke of the war at all. Not to me."

She remembers that grey morning, waiting for him to come home. Standing with Jane in the hall, holding her hand, waiting. And the door banging, and Father coming in. Alice dropping Jane's hand, suddenly terrified that the change that had come over her and Jane in her Father's absence would be obvious. She had never cared about the servants. Let the servants think what they would. But Father. Father could always read her face.

But he seemed to barely see either of them.

"Do you remember," Alice says, taking Jane's hand under the table, "a few days after he came home, that garden party in Winchester for all of the men who'd come home in His Majesty's service?"

"I do. The men were all so quiet. Demoralized at the outcome of the war, I thought. That poor man with the wooden leg who seemed as nervous as a mouse. And the Colonel—"

"And Father, yes."

Overhead, a stomp of feet and creak of floorboards. The Chamber of Commerce meeting sounds boisterous.

They both sit in silence, remembering the argument Colonel Payne had with a fellow officer. It had to do with some soldier who'd been promoted despite not having the seniority or experience that Colonel Payne thought appropriate. Alice had taken her father home, red-faced, stinking of spirits, his vituperation spent, his hands quivering.

It was that week when Alice had determined to do what she must to make their home safe for herself, for Jane, and yes, even for Father himself. She'd keep the gossips and the debtors at bay, and find a way to repair the roof, and step between Father and whichever member of the household he was vilifying. Father tried to keep up their social status, inviting the local men for hunting parties and dinners, while Alice put off the ones she could and tried to make sure there were guns and dogs and fowl when she could not.

"Ah," says Jane, gazing out the murky window. "That must be our Captain King. Let's stop him at the door."

Charles King is as bright and lithe as a flower, his pale green breeches leaving little to the imagination, rising to a close-fitting magenta waistcoat, buttoned high to a bunch of lace at his throat. Even his sage silk coat is tailored slim. He wears a high periwig as white as his skin, and has a chapeau bras under his arm. The only sign that he's a sailor is in his wide stance, nothing like the crossed ankles that should go along with silk stockings and buckled shoes of such magnificence.

Behind him stands a small, stout white man dressed in the more typical American colours, holding a large two-sided bag.

Alice and Jane leap to their feet and to his side. Jane bobs a short curtsy and Alice nods her head.

"Good afternoon, madam, and sir," says King, with hardly a hesitation after looking Alice up and down. "May I be of some assistance?"

"Captain Charles King, I believe?" Jane asks.

His expression turns suspicious. "Zounds, has someone sent you?" His voice drops low. "Have you come from *New Jersey*?"

Alice scowls. One day, she'll need to learn what's behind this fascination with New Jersey.

"You've just sailed from Charleston," Alice supplies. "With letters from the officers there."

He raises an eyebrow. "You seem to know more about my manifest than I do, sir."

"We know something you do not," says Jane. "We know that the mailbag was in the possession of a man who is now under quarantine for smallpox. Do you have any crew members ill?"

He steps back, frowns. "I—my crew has all had that distemper long ago, or been inoculated. We do not carry the bloody pox, and I will not be quarantined."

"Please, sir," says Jane, putting her hand on King's arm. "We don't ask for the ship to be quarantined. Only that you burn those letters."

He glances back at the bag in his servant's hands. "I'm not a man who can afford to make more enemies, madam. I've sworn to deliver those letters to the Merchants, and here I am. If you'll be so kind as to step aside."

He tries to step between them, but Alice steps in, cuts him off.

He puts his hand to the ridiculously ornate sword at his waist. "I warn you. It has been three weeks since I last drank a decent cup of coffee. And I would not scruple to duel a man in uniform."

Alice is almost beyond caring. There are so many scraps of cloth and bits of humanity carrying smallpox from one end of this continent to the other. Who can say whether this mailbag will make anyone sick? But Jane's face has its familiar look of quiet determination about it, her lips bunched and her brows lowered, just as when she's trying to work out some obscure experiment that no one will write about in any journal and no one will ask about in any salon.

Alice swallows. "Captain King, I propose a solution. My companion here will swear that she saw someone steal the mailbag from your servant in the street, here and now. Surely no one will blame you. And I will pay you for your trouble."

"Well," says the captain, his expression softening. "It certainly has been a great deal of trouble . . ." He looks up, past them, toward the sea. "What in God's name?"

The sky is darkening, as if it's about to rain, but the air does not feel damp.

"A storm approaching," says Jane.

He shakes his head. "There's no storm. *Was* no storm, at least. But look at those clouds now. As thick as apple cider, and the same colour too. And it's not yet noon."

He puts a hand to his smooth chin.

It's as dark as twilight now. Children come out into the street and women point at the sky. A bearded man, ragged in his clothing, comes running through the street, yelling, "The time is at hand!"

Darkness is an inadequate word for the oppressive blanket that seems to choke the air. A dog whimpers and scurries, and Alice looks up the street to see how Magpie is faring, but she can't tell from this distance, and in this darkness. A night without stars, a day without sun. Alice shivers, despite her father's heavy coat.

"Something's not right," Alice says, pulling Jane aside.

"A storm," Jane says, her face uncertain.

Charles King and his servant have walked a few yards away from them, toward the sea, to get a better look at the open sky. It's nearly as dark as night now, and a dog bays not far away.

"Let's shimmer away from here," Alice whispers. "Take this bag out to an island and burn it, and then go home."

"I suppose we can always leave a guinea for Captain King later. All right."

Jane sets the time-wheel, while Alice gingerly grasps the mailbag.

"Beloved, now," Alice whispers.

"Yes, I'm trying."

"Now!" Alice whispers, hoarsely, as the sailor turns back to look at them.

"It won't work! I can't make it work. I can't shimmer."

CHAPTER SEVENTEEN

The Black Spot

2145

"When Arthur of Brittany made his *miraculous* escape from the castle at Rouen," Almo says, "at first we thought the Misguideds had opened a new front, but it didn't seem like their style. White princeling in the thirteenth century? Nah. This stank like a Farmer dark mission, but the thing is, Prudence, there are no missions so dark that I don't know about them."

"You want me to confess? I confess."

He grins. "No need, Prudence. I've already caught you. We had the historians take a look at other places that showed some evidence of possible rogue activity. You know the kind of thing: the *Mary Celeste,* the Babushka Lady, Monsieur Chouchani, Gil Pérez... A mysterious appearance or disappearance that wasn't one of our own, or wasn't one we knew to be Misguided activity. At each of these places, we laid a trap. Something that would bring the time travellers to a moment where they could save the life of one of Marcus Larsen's ancestors. And the moment they did—"

Almo claps his right hand over his left, palm-to-palm, like the jaws of an alligator. Prudence flinches.

"What the hell have you done," she says, more threat than question.

"They're fine. They're alive. We thought it would be *you*, you see. But we got your acolytes, and that's fine too. They've allowed us to demonstrate one of our newest technologies. Want to see?"

Either the question is rhetorical or he takes her side-eye as consent. He types a command on the top of his desk and a 3-D image of planet Earth appears above it.

"Interactive light software," he says. "Watch: it changes pretty quickly. This is already Stone Age. Actual satellites, so it's accurate."

This Earth is cloudless, so she can see the edges of the landmasses shifting. Once in a while, there's a big change in the shape of a coastline, and grey masses appear, more and more. Cities.

"It's showing the timeline. From when to when?" She can't help it; she's curious.

"Depends. You can change the settings."

"And—wait. Interactive?"

She glances at his face, and he's wearing a shit-eating grin.

"Interactive. Here, I'll start it earlier this time. Watch Antarctica closely. Should be a few seconds away."

She frowns at the globe. "Where? Oh." A patch of darkness appears over much of Antarctica, a perfect circle, faint at first but it quickly darkens, like a stain.

Almo presses something on his keyboard. "I'll pause it there."

"What the hell is that?"

"Officially, it's called a shroud. I call it the Black Spot. It interferes with time travel in and out of a certain area on a given date. It's going to win the war for us. But first, it helped us make sure that we had our rogues where we could see them, and that you would come home to us."

"You can freeze time travel now? How?"

Almo inclines his head. "For short periods, and within a given area. About the size of a small-to-medium country, for about a day. There are certain . . . side effects. Strange dark weather, but nothing that can't be explained away as an eclipse or a storm or something. Best used in primitive periods, prehistory, you know? It's not something we plan to use much, but now that the Misguideds know we have it, we won't have to use it. Deterrence. We'll finally put an end to this war, Prudence. And I want you here, at the end, to make sure we win it well."

He's not actually content with changing the timeline;

he's going to make sure no one else can change it either. It's brilliant. It could win the war. But God help them if they screw something up.

"Are you telling me my friends are in Antarctica? When?"

He shakes his head. "This isn't the Black Spot in question. We've used it a few times now. The one where your friends are trapped is a different time and place. They can't shimmer out."

She looks back at the globe. "OK, but they could . . . take a bus, and then shimmer, right? What am I missing?"

He barks a laugh. "The Black Spot doesn't just disable time-travel devices temporarily. Once it hits, those devices are bricks. Permanently."

Damn.

She shakes her head. "So there's no way to get them out. But I can stop them from going in the first place. Or get them out after."

Almo shrugs. "Seems unlikely you can manage the first one without a causality glitch, but you're welcome to try. They're there now, you see. Space-time is frozen in that shape, always." He shoots her another shit-eating grin. "I'm sure you're willing to watch a man die, watch his descendants wink out of existence just so you get to have a big sister. I can understand that. But even if you manage it, Prudence, that's not the point."

"It's not?"

He comes out from behind the desk, and she takes a step back, involuntarily.

"The point, Prudence, is that we can always find you. We can always stop you. There is no point to striking out on your own." He casts his gaze downward, his voice softer, sympathetic. "I know how disappointing it was for you to have to redo that nineteenth-century mission of yours so many times, and to no avail. But that's not ever going to happen again. We have new tech. Come back to us, and we'll make sure that what you do sticks."

She shakes her head, but more out of confusion than dissent. "I can't believe you would do all this to get me back. What am I missing here, General? You used who knows how many agents in the field, and who knows how much money and energy on some new weapon, just to get me back? Frankly, I'm not that important."

"No, you're not important at all," he agrees.

"Well, fuck you too."

"You're not. I'm not. Nobody is. That's the point of this, Prudence. You're not learning the lesson; you *are* the lesson. It's a lesson for all our agents that we—the TCC—is the only thing that matters."

She has a vision of a globe of blue and green light, darkening bit by bit, until the timeline is utterly blotted out. No longer this gorgeous, flexible, living thing, but a cauterized wound in the universe.

"You're wrong."

"It's not an opinion, Prudence; it's fact. Your sister, like any other human or plastic fork or oak leaf on this planet, was the result of a million events that could have gone any other way. The individual has no inherent existence. A human life is ephemeral. A conjunction of cause and consequence. Each of us is just . . . information. And one piece of information is not any more valuable than any other. If time travel has taught me anything, it's that individuals don't matter."

"If that's what time travel has taught you, sir," someone says, "then you are a rotten student."

Auden's voice! She whirls and sees him, in his breeches and waistcoat, approaching from the direction of the paper screen. He must have come through the shimmer after her, damn him.

"What the hell—" she begins, just as Almo says, "Who the hell—"

"I'm afraid I shan't give you my name, sir," says Auden, nodding his head in greeting.

He steps in close to her, speaks softly. "Miss Zuniga, if I might—I don't want to touch your belt without your consent—"

She whispers. "I can deal with this myself, Captain."

"I know where to go. I know where they are." His voice

is hoarse, his breath warming her cheek.

She rolls her eyes. Almo is saying something, but it feels a million miles away, as though she and Auden are already in another place and time. She gives Auden an infinitesimal nod, and he steps in close, reaches to her hip and a shimmer opens behind him. He takes both her hands and steps backward, pulling her with him.

CHAPTER EIGHTEEN

Time Is Short, or, a Scheme Is Hatched

1780

"I'll call her Magpie," Alice says.

Jane makes a face. "You are taking her home, then?"

"I don't see why not. Havoc and Thunder could stand a little change, lest they become grumpy old men."

On the inside of Alice's dragoon helmet, a bit of leather stretches, a kind of handle. She runs the horse's rope through it, then freezes at the sight of Jane's face. She follows Jane's gaze.

A shimmer has opened, a few steps from them.

Auden tumbles out backward, with Prudence following, wearing an expression even more wary than her usual.

"Good God," Alice says. "You came after us."

Captain Auden frowns at her. "Miss Payne, is that the Colonel's uniform?"

"A lark," she says, blushing under his censure.

"But how did you know we'd be here?" Jane asks. "*We* didn't even know we'd be here, when we left."

"Yes," says Prudence. "How *did* you know, Captain?"

"I remember the Day of Darkness well enough," Captain Auden says. "Although it did not stretch as far as Charleston, where I was, we heard many stories about that morning. Your General Almo spoke of strange weather, and in my mind's eye I saw my own hand writing the date it happened—you aren't the only one who keeps a diary, Miss Zuniga—May 19, 1780."

Prudence puts a hand up to stop Alice's questions. "But New England is a big place. How did you know they'd be here? Where are we, anyway?"

"New York," Jane says.

"He said Miss Hodgson and Miss Payne would stop a murder in a coffeehouse. So I thought of coffeehouses that would have been dark on this day, and the first one that came to mind was the Merchants, naturally. I thought we might as well start here, and go somewhere else if I missed my guess."

"A murder?" Alice says. "Who told you this?"

Prudence shakes her head. "There's no time to explain. All we know is that this is a trap. We have to get out, or the time-wheel will be destroyed."

She puts her hand to her waist.

"But Miss Zuniga, if we allow this man to be killed," Auden says, "your sister—"

"Never mind that. Don't buy into his games." Prudence opens the shimmer, back to Fleance Hall and 1789. "Let's all go home."

Alice steps backward. "I'm not going anywhere until you explain. We're here to stop a man named Charles King from dropping off a mailbag infested with smallpox at the Merchants Coffeehouse."

"Charles King!" Auden lets out a low whistle. "So that's it. I knew the man. He'd weathered several attempts on his life, and I would not be shocked in the least to discover that one was successful, in some timelines at least."

"You don't remember learning of his death," Prudence says, slowly. "But you do remember the Day of Darkness?"

Captain Auden frowns. "It's possible I would not have heard about his death, I suppose. I don't remember ever meeting him after the siege of Charleston, but everything was such chaos in the war. The last time I remember someone mentioning his name—"

He stops, looks up, stares at Jane as if studying her face.

"Captain Auden," Alice murmurs, impatiently.

"It was you," Captain Auden breathes. "Miss Hodgson. At the battlefield. You were the one who stopped us—" He stops, inclines his head.

"What is this?" Alice looks from Jane to Captain Auden and back again.

Jane shakes her head slightly. "Later, please, Alice."

"I am in your debt, Miss Hodgson," Captain Auden says gravely. "But I fear that your intervention may have alerted Miss Zuniga's former colleagues to your presence. They laid a trap for you, to bring you here. Those soldiers you overheard—I suspect one at least was working for General Almo. I'd wager the murdered man is Charles King. You are meant to speak with him, to delay him, perhaps, or keep him out of the coffeehouse."

"To save his life," says Jane.

"And—?" Alice asks, placing one hand on Prudence's forearm, to tell her to wait, to show her that she is not alone in this, whatever this may be.

"To change history in such a way that Prudence's sister is never born."

"It's already done," Prudence says, her voice a little strangled. "I already don't remember her. They set the chain of events in motion when they set the trap for you. And the moment you save his life, the Black Spot begins. It will prevent you, or anyone, from shimmering out. We'll all be stuck here, for good. So we can't save his life."

"No," says Jane. "But we can make him disappear."

"Given the alternative, I'm sure Mr. King would prefer that plan," says Captain Auden.

"That ought to have the same effect on the future, wouldn't it?" Jane asks. "Your sister would still live?"

Prudence shrugs. "Who can say? It might. But it doesn't matter. The moment Almo realizes what we've done, he'll make Grace disappear some other way. Or he'll just kidnap her the old-fashioned way. Hold her hostage. Get to me that way. Or if we take her, he'll grab her husband, her child, and do to her what he's done to me. He's staked his whole reputation, the reputation of the Farmers, on making sure everyone knows how powerless and insignificant I am. He thinks he's already won. That's why he's not here, now. He wants me to see, to admit, that it's impossible. But if I try to change that, he'll make damn sure to get in my way. He won't give up."

They all hang their heads for a moment.

"It's all right," Prudence says. "Not everyone gets to have a sister. Not everyone gets to live. Forget about it."

Jane shakes her head, holds out her hand, palm down, as if telling the world to be quiet while she thinks. It's a familiar gesture, and Alice smiles despite everything, but it's a sad smile. *Not everyone gets to have a sister,* Prudence said, and Jane heard that. Jane, who lost her own sister not long ago.

"The moment he realizes," Jane repeats. "And if we chose not to give him a moment? We have two ways to shimmer: the belt and the time-wheel. Charles King goes through one, and Grace Zuniga comes into existence in that instant. And in the next instant, Grace goes through the other shimmer, safe from harm. We don't give your General Almo any time to think."

Prudence frowns. "We'd have to get Grace, Alexei and the kid through the shimmer. The best day would be . . . Hmm. The day Nick was born, but before the birth. Only day I know of when my diary says they were in the same place together at a given time. I suppose it could work, but Almo always has a plan B, and a plan C, and a plan D. So long as he can shimmer, he'll come after us." Her eyes widen. "Unless . . . He can't shimmer. All right. OK. I have an idea. But I'll need someone else to get my sister, and someone here, with King. We all have to work fast. Almo thinks quickly."

"Not as quickly as I can ride." Alice cocks her thumb in the direction of Magpie and gives Prudence the smile of a highwaywoman.

CHAPTER NINETEEN

On Captain Auden's Conscience

1780

Wray barely hears his companions; he registers the rise in their voices, the excitement of a new plan. But he cannot tear his eyes away from the piebald horse hitched to the post near the conduit. A rope connects the halter and the conduit, and hanging from the rope is a helmet, tilted just to one side, and within that helmet is a kerchief. Green, and torn, and he is certain he sees the dark brown bloodstains whose pattern he knows so well.

It is, he tries to tell himself, a common enough colour in a handkerchief.

That is Colonel Payne's helmet, certainly. It would be easier—though certainly not pleasant—to believe that the Colonel himself had been the Holy Ghost, all this time. But Wray cannot make himself believe that either. The crumbling edifice that was Colonel Payne, in these last years, could not have been the terror of Hampshire.

It is the handkerchief belonging to the Holy Ghost, a person of daring and good horsemanship, a person who has access to marvelous devices and inventions. A person who concentrates their efforts on the roads of Hampshire, and on gentlemen—he sees it now, the pattern springing into his mind as clearly as stains on cloth—gentlemen of rotten character. A person who came from an embarrassed estate, whose father had debts.

He should have seen it before.

In the dim distance beyond the helmet, he catches another sight: a sight he has not seen for nearly a decade now. The bright green coat and tall peruke that can belong to no other sailor but the man they seek.

Slowly, slowly, he forces himself to look again at Miss Payne. She has followed his gaze to the horse and the rope and the helmet, and the handkerchief within. She swallows, but holds her face steady.

"He's here," Wray manages. "Charles King."

"Jane," Prudence says, clipped and precise, military. "You still have the time-wheel. Take Captain Auden. Go to 2071. There's no time to waste. The second that any one of us talks to Charles King, delays him, anything, we might change the timeline here, and they'll know, and the shroud will descend. Alice, you saddle up."

Alice's chin juts out just a little. "If Captain Auden has

no objection."

Jane, standing beside Alice, takes her hand. Just a catching of the fingers, so subtle it might go without notice.

There is nothing subtle about the reaction from Prudence. "What the actual—Alice, you don't need his permission—"

Wray holds up a hand, his body moving on its own as if it knows already what he has decided. And hasn't he? He can't arrest Alice here and now, and allow Charles King to die, and allow Prudence to live the rest of her life with a guilt-fed empty grief with no memory in it. If a reckoning must come, let it come later. He knows what he must do, now, in this moment.

"Ride, Miss Payne," he says. "There's not a moment to lose."

CHAPTER TWENTY

Containing Sundry Curious Events

2145

Prudence is slightly disappointed by the knowledge that Almo will never live through those thirty seconds of wondering whether she's coming. He'll never have a chance to let the wheels of his terrifying brain run to his plan B, his plan C, whatever they are. He'll never look up, slightly discombobulated, and see her appearing after all, deliberately late.

Still, she did see him do that, and she will always now be thirty seconds wiser for it.

She touches her belt and opens the shimmer into his doorless office at noon, November 30, 2145. She's never even learned where on Earth this office is; it's one of very few pieces of space-time hard coded in to the TCC shimmer belts. And there he is, expectant. He looks slightly satisfied to see her, and slightly wary, as though expecting a trick.

She opens her arms wide, weaponless. "I'm here."

1780

Alice, still in New York, settles into the saddle that is not her own. It smells not only of horse, but of the unknown man whose horse this was. An American; a patriot, he would have called himself. And if Captain Wray Auden had faced him on the field, they would have tried to kill each other.

She has risked her life countless times, out on the road. The risk she is taking now feels different: like a trap closing, like sharp fingers wringing her guts. Captain Auden's face, looking at her as though she'd killed his dog. Prison, first, and then the gallows. Transportation, perhaps, if she can find a way to plead her belly. She smiles, wondering what Jane's eyebrows would do at the notion of an invented pregnancy.

There is some version of Captain Auden that will choose to see her hang for her crimes. Even if a version of her beloved Jane had not told her this, Alice would know it in her heart. The question is whether this Auden will make that choice.

It hurts, deeper than she would have thought, to be reminded that he is only her friend because he doesn't know her. Not all of her. She has let herself be lulled by the veneer she created. She finds that she is grieving, already, for her friendship with him, false though it might have been. They won't play billiards again; he won't lean against the mantel in her drawing room and ask her advice on some historical mystery he is determined to solve.

Damn his eyes! Why must he be so unbending in everything he does? So singular in his understanding of truth and justice? He doesn't know anything about it. There is so much he can't understand.

Magpie shuffles under her, restive. Alice wheels her around in a tight alleyway, where they can watch the road. From here, she can see the hitching stone where they all gathered a few moments ago, but now it's empty. Her friends are gone; Jane is gone; Alice is alone. She has neither belt nor time-wheel but she has a warm horse under her arse and the world before her. There is the small matter of the year, and an ocean, but she has her freedom, for the moment. And isn't that everything she's always wanted? Freedom to make her own life, as she sees fit?

She would find Jane again, surely. Some version of Jane, in some place, in some time. But there would always be a version of Jane whose face would bear the pain of her abandonment. Some version of Prudence who would be caught in a trap of her own making, never knowing the sister she will suddenly remember again.

Does any of it matter?

All things are true, might be true, have never been true.

Knowing that makes the warmth of Magpie's neck, the flare of her nostrils, no less real. This life is all there is, all there ever is.

Alice sits taller in the saddle and peers forward to get a better look at the man on the dock. A formidable wig; clothing in hummingbird hues; a bunch of lace at his throat. That can only be Charles King. He is walking toward the Merchants—he is moments away from death—and her friends are still nowhere to be seen.

She leans forward and whispers in Magpie's ear.

2071

Jane steps through the shimmer into 2071 and Captain Auden follows. There is the strange pedestal, just as Prudence described.

"And now?" Jane says, turning to him.

"And now we wait, I suppose."

Can he be so obtuse? "I mean Alice."

Captain Auden takes a deep, audible breath through his nose, and lets it out, his shoulders sagging. "Have you known all along, Miss Hodgson?"

When it began, it did not feel like the beginning of something. It was a lark, a lesson, an experiment. Revenge on a lecherous pianoforte instructor. "I've known, yes, and I've abetted. If you are going to take Alice to the magistrate, you will have to take me as well."

He runs his hand through his sandy hair, so that the queue in the back shakes violently and the black ribbon tying it nearly comes loose. "But why, Miss Hodgson? Why, in God's name?"

She gives him the most honest answer she can muster, out of honest affection for him. But it takes her a moment to find the words. "You may call it money, if you like."

"Ah."

But she isn't finished. "The Americans began by calling it taxes, didn't they? And they ended by calling it freedom. What it is, Captain Auden, is power. The French are killing each other in the streets over it. You went to America to kill men over it. Alice and I have killed no one. We have merely taken a small amount of power from men who have too much, and put it to our own use in our little corner of Hampshire as best we might."

"No," he says, shaking his head, imperilling the hair

ribbon again. "No, Miss Hodgson, I must disagree. I fought to uphold the law. To prevent the world from falling into an anarchy where any man with a gun may make his own rules."

She puts her head to one side. "Well. Not everyone agrees with the rules, I suppose."

He throws up his hands. "You have so many talents! Both of you. Surely you could put them to better use than robbing—"

Her breath rises in her chest, her rage surprising her. "And what uses do you suggest, Captain? Shall I publish the results of my experiments in small and grubby pamphlets that no one will read? Shall Alice trick a man into marrying her to keep the roof on Fleance Hall? Shall we content ourselves with taking tea with the Bluestocking Society and knitting for the church bazaar?"

He's right, damn him, he's right. But what does he know about it?

And he's ignoring her. Looking past her. She turns to follow his gaze, and sees that in lieu of the pedestal, there's a tent bearing the address T30.

"The timeline," he says. "It's changed. Charles King is . . ."

"No longer alive in New York City," she finishes. "One way or the other."

2145

"Eighteenth century," Almo says, looking Prudence up and down. "1785, give or take. Am I right?"

She forces a tight smile. "You're always right, sir."

He cocks his head, smiles at her, a real smile, or as close to it as he can manage. "No, I'm not. I was wrong to let you get so invested in that nineteenth-century mission. I was wrong to ignore your thoughts about going earlier, going deeper. I thought I'd lost you for good. But then—"

"But then Arthur of Brittany disappeared," she supplies. "And you realized I was using time travel. That I'd gone rogue."

He nods. "And now?"

"Now I've come back. I want my sister back, sir. I don't . . . I don't remember her, but I wish I did. And I've come to understand that I can't accomplish anything on my own."

"But you're not on your own," he says softly. "You've been working with naïfs."

She swallows, nods. "Dumbest mistake I ever made. They don't know what they're doing. They're reckless. Don't understand consequences. I screwed up, sir."

It was Almo himself who taught her that the best way to lie is to tell most of the truth. She steps closer to him, her right hand hanging close to her belt.

2071

The Prudence Zuniga who is with her sister in 2071 puts her hands on her hips and stops Wray and Miss Hodgson from entering the tent.

"Miss Hodgson, Captain," she demands, scowling. "What's happening?"

Wray stops, tries to think. She knows them. She's already deserted the Farmers, already come to live in 1789. But this Prudence calls Miss Hodgson "Miss Hodgson." Early, then. Her desertion is still fresh, her acquaintance with the people of Fleance Hall and its environs still new.

It's strange to see her in drab trousers and a round-necked shirt, yet it suits her, somehow. Wray shakes his head. "There is no time to explain, but you sent us here to take your sister and her family to safety."

Her scowl deepens. "I'm not letting you take her anywhere."

"Damn straight," comes Grace Zuniga's voice, and she steps beside her sister, holding her pregnant belly.

"You gave us a password," Miss Hodgson says. "Juniper."

A shock passes over Miss Zuniga's face, and vanishes again. "Safety. Safety from what? Is something happening here? And why didn't I come myself, if it's so urgent?"

"You are needed elsewhere, Miss Zuniga," Wray explains. "We've given you the password. You must believe that we come from you."

"You could have got that somehow. You could be anyone."

God above, but she's stubborn.

He steps closer to her. "On your arm, there is a tattoo, of a seedling. You told me once . . ."

"What? What the hell did I tell you?"

His face twitches. This is not a comfortable conversation, with everyone else looking on. "That you have never been able to keep plants alive. That you fear—" He stops there, doesn't finish the sentence. Miss Zuniga's amber eyes hold his gaze for a moment. She believes him, now.

"What's the threat?" she asks, less belligerent now. "What's going on?"

Miss Hodgson says, "General Almo is about to erase your sister out of existence."

Grace Zuniga makes an exasperated expression. "I've told you, Prudence, I won't—"

Prudence Zuniga holds up a hand. "Grace, if you go, the baby never exists either. Go. Get Alexei from the back and go."

Grace closes her eyes, takes a deep breath.

"And what happens to you, Prudence?"

"I guess I'll find out."

1780

Charles King walks terribly quickly, despite his high heels. Alice waits, the reins in her right hand, her left free to help Prudence.

But Prudence has not arrived.

The moment has come; the moment has nearly passed. Alice can wait no longer.

Magpie responds to her like powder to a spark, cantering smoothly down the middle of the road, and there, there at last is the shimmer opening, just beside her. A man stumbles out through it, as if pushed, and lands on his hands and knees.

This must be General Almo.

And there is Prudence, behind him. She runs ahead of Magpie, and Alice slows Magpie to a trot as Prudence clambers up onto the hitching stone, and crouches, ready.

This is the moment when everything could fail. Alice breathes, keeps her fear out of her muscles and her pulse, for Magpie's sake. She guides the horse to the hitching stone, feels Prudence's right arm around her shoulders as Prudence's left grabs the pommel, and Prudence's weight suddenly on the horse behind her.

"Go!" Prudence shouts in her ear. But Magpie is already at a canter, and then a gallop, running toward Charles King.

The shimmer opens just beyond him, between him and the door of the Merchants Coffeehouse. The poor man looks up, sees that he's about to be run down, and runs. Not into the road, but toward the coffeehouse. Into the shimmer.

Alice turns Magpie into it as well, and looks behind, sees General Almo running after them.

Then they're through, and Magpie nearly tramples Charles King after all, who find himself in the main hall of Alice's home in 1789. Alice pulls her back, the hooves striking the chequerboard floor.

Prudence closes the shimmer, but whirls to look at it anyway, as if afraid Almo might come through it.

On the other side of the hall, another shimmer opens, and four people come through. Jane, beautiful Jane, as calm as a summer day. A white man with a short golden beard, and a very pregnant woman in trousers.

"Prudence," the woman groans. "Other Prudence. Later Prudence? I'm glad it was really you, anyway. But you'd better damn well know what you're doing. This baby's coming. Alexei?"

"I'm on it," the man says. "We're going to need some privacy. Somewhere where whoever owns this house won't mind some blood."

And Captain Auden, who looks up at Alice, in her borrowed uniform, on her borrowed horse. He is not smiling, but he says, "You did it."

"We did it," Alice counters, as Captain Auden offers Prudence a hand to dismount.

CHAPTER TWENTY-ONE

A Dinner Party and What Comes After

1789

A week after the baby is born, and four days after her father is buried, Alice asks the cook to make a cold supper and lay it in the saloon, the long room up on the top floor of the house that occupies the same footprint as the entrance hall below.

It hasn't been much used, this room, as her father left the top floor to the use of Alice and Jane, and they had little need of this part of it. Today, though, Alice wanted a different place. A place for not quite family, and not quite guests. The saloon is both spacious and private, tucked away up at the top of the house, and people can eat at the five little round tables scattered through it, more comfortably than at the grand table in the dining room downstairs.

The room is old-fashioned, the walls covered in faded

brown-and-yellow tapestries and the ceiling in wood panelling, and the overall effect is too warm, too suffocating. She will have this room redecorated.

Still, it's a good enough place to gather on this extraordinary evening, the first evening when all the residents of Fleance Hall are recovered enough from illness and grief to sup together: Grace Zuniga and her baby and husband, and the young man Arthur, who is well enough now to sit up and eat in company. A decision will have to be made, but for tonight, he's here.

Charles King is recovering from nothing but extreme surprise and has been a whirlwind of activity Fleance Hall can barely contain, but there is nowhere else for him to go, at present, so Captain Auden has been occupying him with conversation. Captain Auden is here tonight too, the only person in the room who is not resident at Fleance Hall, although he might as well be.

Grace Zuniga and her husband don't sit at a table at all but on a settee, picking at stewed fruit, nuts and bread, while Grace cradles her baby son. Prudence paces behind them, pausing in her path only when Alice interrupts it, hands her a glass cup of rum punch.

"We're all still here," Alice says.

Prudence nods. "It's been a week. I keep expecting Almo to knock on your doors, nine years older and nine years meaner, having crossed the Atlantic in a ship. But he hasn't. Maybe he's mellowed. Maybe he died. Or maybe he found a TCC safe house and they figured out a way to let him shimmer again. I don't know anything about this weapon they've developed, this shroud. The Black Spot, he called it. What an ass. I don't like it."

She looks up, across the room, and smiles. It's a rare sight, and Alice follows her gaze, to the table where three men sit in strange conversation: the medieval princeling Arthur, a hunk of cold beef in his hand; Charles King, powdered to high heaven and sipping his punch with an arch expression; and Wray Auden, his own expression inscrutable.

Alice walks to them, and they all rise. "Please, sit."

But Captain Auden stays standing, as if restless, and joins her at a little distance from the table. His face is even more animated than usual, a pregnant stillness that she can't interpret.

She asks the boy Arthur, in her slowest and most careful French, whether he is feeling well, and he inclines his head, says something in response she can't quite understand.

"His Royal Highness is nearly completely recovered," Captain Auden supplies.

"And he truly wishes to stay . . . here?"

Captain Auden's face goes pink. "The information Prince Arthur has, about the course of history in the twelfth century, does not lead him to want to return."

"I see," says Alice, with one corner of her mouth twitching to a grin at *the information Prince Arthur has.* "We must all make decisions about what seems most just, when our principles clash. Speaking of which, Captain, I did not have an opportunity to thank you for your presence at my father's funeral, and for allowing me the time and freedom in which to bury him."

"There is no reason to thank me, Miss Payne."

"I can't help but notice, Captain Auden, that I am still at liberty. May I assume this will be a permanent condition? I believe Jane kept the shackles from your medieval adventure. I can have her fetch them now for me, if you'd like."

He swallows. "I have resigned my post as parish constable, Miss Payne. It seemed the only path open to me. The only path I was willing to take, rather."

"I'm sorry to hear that," she says sincerely, her battle-grin dropping. "You were a magnificent constable. Truly. What will you do with your newfound leisure, Captain Auden?"

A small snort that might be a laugh. "New House needs my attention, as does the farm. I think I shall invite your Dr. Jenner to come and have a conversation with my milkmaids. Miss Hodgson is keen to encourage him to keep exploring the connection between cowpox and smallpox."

"And what will Prudence say about that, I wonder?"

"She has given me her blessing, as a matter of fact," says Jane, walking over to join them. "I am making plans to hold a regular salon, during which I will encourage England's great men of science in ways that I suspect they will find profitable."

Alice shakes her head. "Your knowledge should be profitable to you, Jane, not to them."

"It will be." Jane slips her arm through Alice's and they look out over the room.

"Good God, this is a motley household, isn't it?" Alice murmurs.

"It is a big old house," Jane says contentedly. "I have a feeling we are going to put it to excellent use."

The Most Recent Draft of History

1756: Alice Payne is born in Kingston, Jamaica

1759: Alice and her father come to England; he buys Fleance Hall

1778: Alice's father goes to America to fight (Alice is 22)

1783: Alice's father returns, wounded

1784: Wray Auden buys New House

1788: The Earl of Ludderworth goes through a time portal

1889: Crown Prince Rudolf dies in the Mayerling Incident

1913: Franz Ferdinand narrowly escapes death while hunting in England

1914: Franz Ferdinand is assassinated and the First World War begins

1916: The Battle of the Somme

2038: Discovery of time travel

2040: Prudence and Grace Zuniga arrive in Toronto as child refugees from the future

2070: Prudence, Helmut and Rati set up Project Shipwreck

2071: Teleosophy begins

2091: The Berlin Convention on Organ Manufacture

2092: The History War begins

2131: Grace is born

2132: Prudence is born

2135: Invention of wireless remote EEG scanning

2139: The Anarchy begins

2140: Prudence and Grace are sent back in time by their parents

2145: Teleosophic Core Command

Acknowledgments

This book is dedicated to my parents, who have been supporters of my writing from the days when it was alarming my elementary school teachers. Their faith and wisdom made everything in my life possible.

It also honours Linda Nicholson-Brown, one of *Alice*'s first and most enthusiastic readers and a woman who brought joy and love to the world.

I'm grateful for the love and support of Linda, Shirley, Brent, Xavier, Ian and Jen, along with the rest of my wonderful family.

My thanks to my editor, Lee Harris, who believed in this book and made it better, and to all those at Tor.com and Macmillan who helped Alice step out into the world.

Hardly a day goes by when I don't thank my lucky stars for the privilege of working with Jennie Goloboy at the Donald Maass Literary Agency.

I'm indebted to Robert Dawson and Brent Warren for reading an early draft. Any errors or oversights are mine alone.

About the Author

KATE HEARTFIELD is a former newspaper editor and columnist in Ottawa, Canada. Her novel *Armed in Her Fashion* (ChiZine Publications) was published in 2018, as was her interactive novel *The Road to Canterbury* (Choice of Games). Her short fiction has appeared in several magazines and anthologies, including *Strange Horizons* and *Lackington's*. Her website is heartfieldfiction.com and she tweets at @kateheartfield.

TOR·COM

**Science fiction. Fantasy. The universe.
And related subjects.**

*

More than just a publisher's website, *Tor.com*

is a venue for **original fiction, comics,** and

discussion of the entire field of SF and fantasy,

in all media and from all sources. Visit our site

today—and join the conversation yourself.